DEADLY DEPOSIT

BY KESLIE PATCH-BOHROD

Published by Starry Night Publishing.Com
Rochester, New York

Copyright 2021 Keslie Patch-Bohrod

D1302257

AUTHOR'S DISCLAIMER

This is a work of fiction. The towns, cities, restaurants, wineries, hotels or any other locations mentioned within this novel are real but used within in a fictional setting. The remaining names, characters, places, and incidents are either a product of the author's imagination or are used fictitiously, and any resemblance to actual persons, living or dead, events or places is entirely coincidental or has nothing to do with their actual conduct. I can personally attest to the exceptional quality and taste of all the food and wine listed and described.

The letter that Jack receives in this story is an actual extortion letter that scammers tailor with the target's name and address. The mistakes within the letter belong to the scammer not me. I cannot give the author of this letter credit for his or her work for obvious reasons, but I doubt I will be charged for plagiarism when they are guilty of a much greater crime.

*****

Thank you to my husband Bill Bohrod, Jayne Rutan (twice!), Carey Schwartz Roseman and Laurie Mortensen for taking the time to read, edit and suggest changes/additions and to the rest of my family and friends for their support and encouragement.

Also by Keslie Patch-Bohrod

Loveladies Ennui (Miranda Craig Thriller #1)

CONTENTS

CHAPTER 1

Labor Day 2018

"What do you mean you don't like the way the dead man got up and walked away?!" screeched an incredulous Miranda Craig.

Over the summer, Miranda and her husband Jack had purchased an apartment building in Somerville, New Jersey as an investment. They had asked Celia Ravenscroft, the property manager, to stay on temporarily until Miranda could decide how involved she wanted to be in the day-to-day operations. Because several trips had been planned for the fall, Miranda knew she would not be available full time until after Christmas when their kids' college winter holiday break was over. The plan was to slowly acclimate herself to the running and managing of the property, under Celia's tutelage. Once Miranda was comfortable with the work and tenants, Celia would then devote all her time to managing Greg Baker's properties throughout Somerset County. The Craigs had purchased this building from him as he was more interested in adding larger complexes to his holdings and this was a smaller building in downtown Somerville that didn't fit his portfolio.

Miranda was stunned by Celia's call during her drive home from Long Beach Island, New Jersey. "This can't be happening! I have had the worst summer on record with Russian spies, murders and nonstop construction noise. Now I have to deal with this?" shouted Miranda.

After a neighbor in their Long Beach Island shore town had died, Miranda began to suspect he had been intentionally killed. Learning of his history, as well as the history of Loveladies, their elite shore community, she uncovered a Soviet plot against the United States. The entire summer had been disrupted by murders, break-ins and espionage. With it finally over, Miranda was looking forward to an uneventful autumn. Shaking her head in disbelief, she pleaded, "Celia, please start from the beginning and tell me everything you know."

Celia took a deep breath and began to tell Miranda about what happened over the Labor Day weekend. "The day started out as usual, phone calls from tenants concerning issues with the valet trash service, questions concerning when the exterminators would be coming next to spray for cockroaches and complaints about crazy phone calls. I couldn't do anything about the last one, so I just recommended they call their phone service provider or maybe get their phone number listed with the National Do Not Call Registry. Then I received a phone call," continued Celia, "from a gentleman named Roger Newman saying he was worried about his friend Allister. That is the name of one of our tenants, Allister Foley. He had, Roger that is, received an email from his friend saying that he was depressed and not happy staying in his new apartment. Although he was initially quite happy with the apartment, Allister changed his mind after meeting his neighbors. They were not friendly in the least; they played their televisions and music at full blast all hours of the night and they would constantly park in the spot designated for his apartment. Then, much to Mr. Newman's dismay, Allister said he couldn't take it anymore. Mr. Newman said that he had been away in England visiting family and was unable to check up on his friend until Labor Day. They had been corresponding for quite some time and the emails, before this one, were always filled with humor, long stories of the wonderful people he was meeting and how he couldn't wait until Mr. Newman returned. Allister wrote of things he planned to do and was always incredibly positive."

"This too, was my impression of Allister every time I spoke with him. He was very friendly and always making jokes. I never received one complaint from him or about him. As you know when you visit here, the tenants are very respectful of one another. I am surprised, no shocked, that he would say that his neighbors were noisy and unfriendly. I have made it a point to outline our expectations here and to stress that we all need to be good neighbors, and anything less will not be tolerated."

"So anyway, you can imagine how worried Mr. Newman became upon his return from abroad and received this uncharacteristic message. He didn't even unpack his bags; he just drove straight to Allister's apartment to check on his friend."

6

"When he got to the apartment, he knocked on the door but there was no answer. He tried the handle and was surprised to find the door was unlocked. Even though it seemed like a good neighborhood, Mr. Newman knew Allister was a cautious man, plus he had some valuable items in his possession. Someone could just walk in and possibly steal from him; he would never take that chance."

"Mr. Newman walked into the living room, then checked the kitchen, bathroom and finally the bedroom where he found his friend Allister lying on the floor beside the bed. He noticed Allister's hand appeared to be quite swollen, the fingers were awkwardly bent and bruised. He was surprised that he had not been informed how badly his friend had hurt himself or how it had happened, even though just receiving an email from him. Checking for a pulse and not finding one, he looked around for a phone. He looked through the nightstand by the bed, kitchen, living room and even the bathroom. There was no cell phone or landline in sight. He reached into his pocket where he usually kept his own cell phone and realized, in his haste to get inside, that he had left it in the car. Knowing time was of the essence, he rushed out the door, down the steps and to his car where he found his phone and called 911. Out of breath, he was barely able to ask for police and an ambulance. He explained to the 911 dispatcher what he found and that he was almost certain his friend was dead. The dispatcher asked him to return to the apartment and check again and remain on the line so she could instruct him on how to begin CPR just in case. When he entered the bedroom again, he was shocked to find it empty."

"So, what are you telling me?" asked Miranda. "That the tenant wasn't really dead and walked away?"

"I don't know what I am telling you," replied Celia. "All I know is that the tenant is no longer there and when I pulled up his information on our system to see if he had listed any contacts in case of an emergency, I found his direct deposit billing had been terminated. Then I called our bank and was informed that yes, he had cancelled further payment and his social security checks were going elsewhere- where, they didn't know. I called the Social Security office to see if they could tell me where he had forwarded his checks, but they told me they were not at liberty to divulge that information. We might have recourse with his heirs if he is dead, but you will need to contact an attorney. I checked with the cable, internet and electric companies and they all told me he was no longer a customer. No forwarding information given. The police, at the insistence of Mr. Newman, have filed a missing person report and are trying to locate him. I just thought you should know what was going on. How do you want me to proceed? Since everything has been cancelled, it appears that he intended to go somewhere else, but he hasn't removed his clothing, furniture or food. Should I clean the apartment and get it ready to be rented? What should I do with his furniture?"

Miranda, trying to drive home from the shore in heavy traffic, couldn't process what Celia was telling her. She needed time to think things through and get a better handle on all the facts.

"Celia, do nothing for the time being. Have the police taped off the apartment as a possible crime scene?"

"No, they found no evidence that a crime had been committed there. There was no blood and no body" reported Celia. "The front door and windows showed no signs of a break-in."

"Did they look for any fingerprints, locate Allister's laptop or cell phone?" asked Miranda.

"Not that I know of," replied Celia.

"Well, I think, for at least the next few days we have to assume that Mr. Foley will be in touch to tell us what his plans are and until then, we can't rent out the apartment or dispose of his furniture. I assume we also have a security deposit that will see us through this waiting period?" asked Miranda.

"Yes, we take a two-month security deposit." responded Celia.

"Our next steps," continued Miranda "will be to wait for the police and Mr. Newman to contact us should they find something, and then we will make a decision on how to proceed. If he really intended to terminate his lease ahead of schedule, we may have to contact an attorney or collection agency because I believe he is still liable for the remaining monthly payments under the rental agreement he signed."

CHAPTER 2

When Celia hung up the phone to Miranda, she wondered if she should call Greg Baker and tell him about the missing tenant. He was no longer the legal owner of the apartment building, but she did still work for him managing the remainder of his properties. He might know something or have some advice on what to do. Surely, he'd had people vacate ahead of their contract. But then again, maybe she would wait until she knew more before bothering him with this. It really didn't impact his business, so waiting would be no big deal.

In deep thought, Celia sat at her desk looking out the window. She hated having to call Miranda about this, especially at the end of a holiday weekend. The poor woman seemed distraught and what was all that talk about Russian spies and noise? God, was this woman going to be a pain in the ass to work with, or was she just having a bad day?

What should she do next? Something about this disappearance did not feel right. Maybe she should knock on some of his neighbors' doors and see if they knew anything. He had been a friendly guy, always chatting with anyone nearby. Someone might have heard or seen something that could give her a clue as to what happened to him.

She closed her computer, locked her office door and took the elevator up to Allister's floor. A few seconds after ringing the next-door neighbor's doorbell, a young woman came to the door. Celia prided herself on knowing all the tenants in this building, which was easy because she alone had rented them the apartments.

Greeting the woman, she began to ask, "Hi Cindy, sorry to bother you, I was wondering if you were around this past weekend? A friend of your next-door neighbor thinks something might have happened to him. I thought I would check with you to see if you might have heard or seen something."

"Are you talking about Allister?" asked Cindy.

Celia nodded in the affirmative.

"Oh no, I hope he's alright, he is such a nice guy. He always tells Bill and me about the new restaurants he tries and makes recommendations to us for our date nights. I wish I could help, but we were visiting Bill's family in Avalon for the weekend. We just got back about an hour ago because the traffic was so heavy. "

"Well, if you see Allister or learn anything about where he might have gone, please call me right away. I am getting worried about him."

Cindy agreed saying, "I sure will. Bill just ran out to the store for a few things for our dinner tonight. When he comes back, I'll ask him if he knows anything, and I will be sure to ask around the building to see if any of the other tenants might know of something."

Celia thanked her, went across the hall, and rang the bell of one of the other neighbors, Stan Little. When no one answered, she figured Stan was at work. He owned one of the restaurants in downtown Somerville and being a busy holiday weekend, she didn't expect him back home any time soon. She put a note in his mailbox asking him to call her later that night or when he had a minute.

Feeling dismayed at not learning anything new, she returned to her office. Had Allister been unhappy? Did he hide what he was really feeling inside by being super cheery on the outside? Being a widower, he was probably lonely. She understood how loneliness made you feel and how it could lead to questionable actions.

CHAPTER 3

Sitting at her office desk, Celia thought how life had finally taken a good turn for her, and now this. The past few years had been horrible. Celia's divorce had been bitter and her self-esteem was shattered. How could her husband be so unhappy with her that he would walk out on a twenty-one-year marriage? But he did. Now he had a young, extremely attractive girlfriend that just increased her pain and added to her low self-worth. In addition, he refused to help with Kim's college tuition and barely spoke with her. It was unfathomable how a father could abandon his own daughter like that.

Was their relationship doomed from the beginning because they got married at such a young age? She was barely out of college when they got married and nine months later, she had Kim. It had been two and a half years since Brian left her and only just recently had she been able to snap back. At forty-four she still had a lot of life ahead of her and she was bound to go after whatever she could get. Kim, a junior and just turning twenty-one, was doing well in college and had encouraged Celia to begin to make a move forward with her life.

It didn't seem that long ago that she was looking through the New Jersey Star Ledger newspaper one Sunday morning in the spring when she spotted a classified ad for an Apartment Manager position. The high rise in Somerville was only a fifteen-minute drive from her apartment in Basking Ridge, which made it ideal. In addition, during college she had been a resident assistant in her dorm and a few years ago she had passed the test for her New Jersey Real Estate license. Because she was outgoing and affable, which were necessary personality traits in the real estate business, she hoped she would have a chance at the job.

Instead of emailing or mailing her resume, she decided she would take a chance and stop by to introduce herself. She always believed the personal touch was important, especially in a customer service type position, like real estate. If she could show the owner how friendly and competent she was, maybe she could land the job.

Donning her best suit, Celia loved how the teal-colored jacket and skirt drew attention to her blue green eyes. A little lip gloss, gold necklace and black leather pumps finished off her outfit. As she gave herself the once over in the mirror, she looked and felt confident.

Downtown Somerville was changing. Over the last few years, it began to mirror some of the more successful downtown areas like Millburn, Summit and Westfield, upgrading buildings' facades and encouraging trendy restaurants, thus revitalizing a previously old, worn-out town.

As she double checked the address in the newspaper ad to the number on the outside of the chic apartment building, a wave of panic struck her. The building looked so high end with its glass and chrome exterior, black awning over the front entrance and large black planters with colorful flowers flanking the double doors.

Deciding she had nothing to lose, and hoping the owner would be there, Celia found the door to the leasing office just inside the entranceway and walked in. That was when she first laid eyes on Greg Baker. He was so handsome and charismatic, just over six feet tall with brown hair and blue eyes. Inviting her to sit down in the chair opposite his desk, he got down to business. He told her about the position and the other apartment buildings he owned in the area. If she proved herself capable, he envisioned her assuming the responsibility of managing additional properties.

They seemed to hit it off right away, chatting about where they were from, the schools they attended, things they liked to do in the area. As she described her work history and skills, his expression seemed to indicate that her experience was sufficient. He showed her around the office where the manager would spend most of the day, then gave her the grand tour of the rental units available, pool and barbeque area, laundry facilities and mail room. As they were walking back to the office, he offered her the job and asked if she would be able to start the next day.

It all happened so quickly. They went back to his office where Greg made his official offer of what her starting salary and health benefits would be. She accepted of course because she really needed a job. Learning how to manage the apartment would not be easy but Greg assured her that he would hold her hand for the first couple of weeks to make sure she got the hang of it; after all, it wasn't rocket science.

Her divorce settlement only provided a minimal income, which irked Celia. She had given up her life for her no-good ex-husband, putting everything on hold for those twenty one years. He had wanted a 'traditional' wife, one that stayed home with the children, cleaned house, ironed his shirts and had dinner on the table at exactly five-thirty when he got home from work.

That life wasn't exactly what she had planned, but she had been determined to make the best of it. The birth of their daughter had been wonderful, and she threw herself into the role of mother. Getting married and having a child at such an early age limited her life experiences. In many ways, she didn't know what she had been missing.

When Kim went away to college and Celia's husband asked for a divorce, her life dramatically changed. There was a huge gap and nothing there to fill it.

Now things were looking up. An income of her own, a good-looking boss and most of all, she would be too busy to feel sorry for herself.

After the second full week of working together, Greg suggested they go for drinks at a nearby restaurant. Since it was a Friday night, he thought it would be a good way to wind down after all the training she had gone through. She knew she shouldn't, but she acquiesced and thought it wise to follow him in her car. That way she could leave at any time should an awkward situation arise.

To her surprise, he pulled up in front of Wolfgang's Steakhouse on Main Street in Somerville. She had heard about how good it was but never had the money to try it. The restaurant was on the main level of one of the newly renovated buildings along Main Street. It had that New York trendy vibe to it, dark wood paneling, leather chairs, white tablecloths and waiters with black aprons rushing around delivering sizzling steaks.

As they made their way to the bar, Greg told her, "They make a great martini here." He pulled out a barstool for her and continued, "You really have to try their homemade potato chips with one."

While they watched their bartender shake their iced classic Martini with gin and a hint of dry vermouth, the bar area started to get crowded. This forced Celia and Greg to move their barstools closer together in order to hear the other speak. Over the past two weeks, Celia had a chance to get to know Greg. He was a driven, successful man and she wondered if he kept himself busy so he wouldn't realize how lonely he was.

Their drinks were poured into tall, stemmed martini glasses and they had to bend over the bar to sip the liquid which was filled to the brim. The hot, fresh potato chips were delivered in an oval wicker basket and Celia could see they were covered with a coarse salt.

She was hooked. The Bombay Sapphire gin was ice cold, and the olives were huge and wonderfully briny. They were an appetizer all on their own. When the bartender delivered the freshly fried chips, she thought she died and had gone to heaven. Savory snacks were her favorite. She laughed to herself now about how she had said an altered line from one of her favorite movies, "You had me at potato chips."

Celia thought he sensed her apprehension about being out with the boss, as he kept the conversation focused on business and what was in store for the next week. It was only when he was seeing her to her car that the mood changed dramatically. He only said, "I'm so glad you walked into my office. If I hadn't hired you, we wouldn't be here right now. I hope you feel the same."

Celia did feel the same and that's what worried her. She was concerned about getting involved with him. Greg Baker seemed like such a nice man, but as they say- you shouldn't get involved with your boss. She had been so lonely living on her own after her husband walked out on her. Then shortly after that, their daughter went off to college in Tampa, Florida and she was all alone. Celia received some alimony through the divorce, but in order to make ends meet and for her own well-being, she knew she would have to find a job. Thankfully, Kim's college education was fully funded because of a trust account set up years earlier by Celia's mother. It even covered Kim's apartment, food and car expenses. Without that financial assistance Kim would not have been able to attend an out of state college. So here Celia was, finally moving her life forward and falling for her boss.

CHAPTER 4

Spring 2018

Greg hadn't seen Mike O'Ryan in twenty something years. They had gone to high school together at Watchung Hills Regional High School in Warren, New Jersey and had been great friends, playing on the school's baseball team. They went in different directions for college; Greg had attended Lehigh University in Bethlehem, Pennsylvania while Mike had opted for Haverford College in Haverford, Pennsylvania. They had both returned to New Jersey after completing their college degrees.

Greg's father had advanced him seed money upon graduation and challenged him to put his finance degree to work. Greg had always had an interest in Real Estate and bought his first apartment building. He skimped and saved until he had enough money for a down payment on a second building. With patience, discipline and hard work, he had been able to acquire eight so far. Apartment buildings were a great way to acquire wealth, because there was a monthly cash flow that helped to make repairs when needed, fund improvements when it was time, and to finance additional properties when a nice bargain popped up in the market. Somerset County was growing and there was a demand for nice, well-priced apartments. Accumulating the properties had been easy for Greg, the hard part was keeping them fully rented.

One Friday night after leaving his office, he decided to go to his usual hangout, Wolfgang's in Somerville, for a drink and dinner at the bar. A Bombay gin martini had just been placed in front of him when Mike O'Ryan came in. They hadn't seen each other since high school. Mike immediately ordered a drink and sat down next to Greg, shaking his hand and saying, "Oh my God- Greg Baker, you are a sight for sore eyes. You are just the man I would love to commiserate with right now! I just lost a big account and I need someone to get drunk with. Are you with me brother?"

Greg, after having a tough week of trying to get all his units rented said, "I'm your man and it's good to see you too! I don't think I would have recognized you if I didn't hear your voice. You have really changed. Your face has filled out and you have a professional haircut, not that long mess of hair you had in high school."

They sipped their drinks for a few minutes then Greg said, "What have you been doing since college? We kind of lost touch, you know."

"Well," said Mike, "I got an economics degree from Haverford and went to work for my dad for a while in his real estate company managing commercial properties. I got tired of him telling me what to do and how to do it twenty-four seven. I saw a need while I was there and developed a business plan. I launched my own residential rental real estate service. I oversee all the grunt work of finding tenants, qualifying them, vetting them then offering them up to my select clients on a silver platter. All they must do is say 'Thank you, Mike!,' give me a small percentage of the rental income and they get all the rest of the funds direct deposited into their accounts. Most of my clients don't even have a leasing office anymore. All the contracts, reference forms and miscellaneous paperwork for billing are all on my proprietary website and system. Everything is online. All that is needed is a maintenance person or an onsite employee who lives and works out of one of the units and can show the apartments or authorize the move in. In many cases that is just the maintenance person. It is that simple."

"Wow! That's incredible! What are the occupancy rates of your clients?" asked Greg.

"Why, it is almost one hundred percent. We have so many tenants lined up there is very little down time. Since most apartments in this area are basically designed the same way and with the same upgrades, it all boils down to price and location. So that makes my job even easier. A lot of the agreements are signed sight unseen. You've seen one apartment; you've seen them all!"

Greg couldn't believe what he was hearing. If he could get Mike to take on his apartments, he could have so much more time for himself. Right now, he was lucky to have one evening for a drink and dinner. Maybe he could even begin to have a social life. He couldn't remember the last time he went out on a date.

Greg had recently put an ad in the paper advertising for a property manager to deal with the day to day activities that took up so much of his time. With Mike's help, maybe the manager could take on more responsibilities.

Mike finished his drink, ordered another and a Porterhouse steak medium rare for dinner with the trimmings: fried potatoes, creamed spinach and a plate of sliced tomatoes and Vidalia onions. Wolfgang's was Mike's favorite restaurant. It was modeled after the well-known and loved Peter Luger's Steakhouse in Brooklyn and Great Neck, New York. In fact, Wolfgang used to be a waiter there for 40 years. Instead of retiring, he, his son and two others opened their own restaurants, serving very similar foods to the famed Lugers, one of which happened to be in Somerville. Greg liked the sound of Mike's order and asked for the same. He then suggested they take a booth near the bar where they could continue their discussion. Greg was anxious to hear more about Mike's business model and hoped there was a way he could benefit from it.

When their food arrived, they each took bites of their hot steaks and savored the perfectly grilled meat. Greg put his knife and fork down, took a drink of his second martini and said, "Mike, your business sounds like something I could use. I have a number of apartment buildings in the area, and I am struggling just to maintain about a sixty percent occupancy rate. Would you be willing to meet with me next week, look at my units and maybe put together a proposal for me?"

"Greg, I am so happy I ran into you tonight. I would be delighted to take a look. I am sure I can help you out. Let me give you my cell number. Text me tomorrow with a couple of dates and times you are free. We will set something up."

They met at Greg's first apartment building on that next Wednesday. Mike asked for a listing of all of Greg's properties and told him he would visit each then run some numbers. He was glad Greg had photos and leasing information on all of the internet sites like *apartments.com*; it would make his job easier. Mike would just have to replace Greg's phone numbers with his, steering the potential tenants his way to vet them. Greg didn't need to know that he might take a few of these potential tenants for other unconventional if not illegal revenue streams. He could offer Greg a fantastic rate, then really clean up on the side business he was operating.

Mike phoned Greg the next Monday and said he was emailing the proposal as they spoke.

"Greg, just to let you know, I am giving you a lower rate per tenant because of our friendship and the number of units you have. Your volume alone qualifies you for our lower rate. To give you an example, I am charging you a onetime fee of eighteen percent, so that is two hundred seventy dollars for a fifteen hundred dollar a month apartment. If I am able to rent forty units, that will net me ten thousand eight hundred dollars. Then you'll take in an additional seven hundred nine thousand dollars on those rentals for the year. With my business, it is basically a service, so I have very little overhead. I have had time to fine tune my process, so there is very little I have to do to get you up to full occupancy."

Greg couldn't believe his ears. Two hundred seventy a unit was great. He had been spending so much on advertising and marketing brochures and if he didn't need an onsite manager at each location, it would save him even more. Now, he could just use Mike and the few websites that had historically paid off. Over time, he might even be able to do away with those and solely use Mike's services.

"Thanks Mike, that all sounds great. I see the proposal in my email. I will take a look at it right now and if everything looks good, I will print, sign it and drop it off at your office. I want you to get started as soon as possible."

"That's great," said Mike. "I am a full-service kind of guy. Just let me know when you have the signed papers, and I will swing around and pick them up. It is all part of the service."

Greg printed out the contract and began to run his own numbers and projections. With higher occupancies he could afford to buy that new apartment complex in Bridgewater he had been eyeing. It had been on the market only a month and he was anxious to submit an offer.

He desperately needed someone to help manage the properties. He didn't care if that someone was smart, he was looking more for a warm body to answer phones, go to the bank to make weekly deposits, enter data into their system and address the tenant complaints. With the increase in business that Mike promised, he just wouldn't have the time to oversee all of the apartments.

Keslie Patch-Bohrod

CHAPTER 5

Mike O'Ryan could never stand his old man, so when he was forced to go to work in his commercial real estate business after college he knew it wouldn't last long. About six months in, he met Eddie Davis while collecting rents Down Neck for his father. Eddie was working at Newark Penn Station where Mike would catch the train back to Summit to his father's office. Eddie had a news stand near the track where Mike would wait for his train.

They began talking and sharing alternative methods of making a living. Right away, they saw they had similar beliefs and felt an entitlement to the better things in life- regardless of how that was achieved.

Eddie knew a bunch of guys looking for tech work and suggested Mike find a commercial property where they could set up shop. Mike had developed a number of leads he didn't share with his father; one of which was an old strip mall in Bound Brook. He immediately signed a lease and they started in business. This community was perfect not only because it was on the train line and had a Shop Rite, but because of the resident population. There was a significant Hispanic/Latino population he thought he could take advantage of.

Mike developed a number of email, telephone and rental scams and Eddie found and hired the guys to carry it out. Computers and phone systems were set up for thirty or more scammers. The men would sit at their workstations and call unsuspecting targets on a wide range of well-orchestrated pitches. One such scam started by sending out automated robocalls saying there was a problem with their computer that required immediate action, or their computer would fail. The person could be connected with a certified technician who would diagnose the problem and fix it on the spot. If the person requested to be connected, the scammer would ask for access to the computer. Once in the target's computer, the scammer would show meaningless warning messages and convince the person they had a real problem. The cost to fix the problem was given; only a few forms of payment were accepted: gift cards, Bitcoin, cash, Venmo or wire transfer- all untraceable. Mike liked his guys in this scam scenario to focus on people over sixty because they tended to be less tech-savvy.

Not wanting to be a one size fits all criminal, he developed another plan to go after Hispanic undocumented immigrants focusing on their fear of deportation. Pretending to be the Internal Revenue Service, Federal Bureau of Investigation or an agent from Immigration and Customs Enforcement, the scammer would demand money to cover costs that would allow the person to remain in the country.

Mike continued to work for his father for a few more months until he had raised sufficient cash and was able to put together another scheme that dealt with the rental business. That was going well, until it wasn't going well. He decided to take some time to himself and try to figure his next steps.

Mike couldn't believe his luck running into Greg like that at Wolfgang's. The timing couldn't have been better. Greg was anxious to get tenants into his buildings and Mike was desperate to replace Harry Murphy, his former business partner. Harry owned four large apartment complexes in Southern New Jersey and had been very excited with Mike's proposal. The only problem was that Harry was very hands on and kept a close eye on every aspect of his business, including Mike's involvement.

Mike had hoped he would see signs that Harry might be open to some 'extra cash,' but Harry always declined to talk about any shady prospects, as he put it.

Mike had Eddie Davis, his right-hand man, helping out at all the apartments, however, the tenants started to complain to Harry about Eddie's presence around the buildings at all hours of the day and night. Mike tried to explain that Eddie was taking measurements or updating photos of the complex to include nighttime shots, saying that women like to see how well the complex was lighted at night around the laundry rooms, parking lots and entrance ways.

Harry didn't buy it and said he wanted Eddie off his premises. Tenants were complaining of strange phone calls and the number of tenants non-renewing leases seemed to be too high. He had never had these problems before Mike and Eddie got involved with his business which prompted him to look at the numbers and tenancies closer. He was concerned about churning. Could they somehow make people leave early so they could earn the fee on new tenants?

Then last week, Harry told Mike he was thinking of bringing in a forensic accountant to go over his books and leases to confirm with each tenant their lease arrangements. "Something's just not right here. I don't know what it is, but I can feel it. The guy I'm bringing in used to do work with the FBI and can find things you wouldn't believe. I think Eddie is doing something here and I mean to find out what it is."

"Harry, I understand your concerns. I've never had any problems before with Eddie, but I can't let you be unhappy with my service. I will let him go today. Before you hire anybody, why don't you let me look at your books and leases and see if I can find anything? Free of charge," offered Mike. The offer to pull Eddie and look over the financials seemed to appease him. Mike had to find a way to keep Harry happy or quiet.

Some of Harry's apartment buildings were in Monmouth County and others were in Green Brook, part of Somerset County, which also had a substantial Hispanic population. Mike's guys had been heavily cashing in on the ICE ruse when they found out how many undocumented workers were living there with family members or friends. The tenants were complaining to Harry about all these calls that appeared to be from federal agents shaking down those who were believed to be illegally here in the United States. If Harry got wind of who and what they were doing, it would end a very lucrative business for Mike. He could keep Harry happy only for so long. He would need to quiet him soon- very soon.

So, Mike asked Eddie to take care of Harry.

Of course, Eddie understood what Mike was asking him to do. They had been working together for a quite a while now and Mike asked Eddie to do all sorts of things. The implications of those acts were always very clear to Eddie. He may look like he didn't understand but he did. He may not be a member of MENSA, but he could spell it.

Eddie said he knew a guy, who knew a guy, who knew a guy's cousin that could help him make Harry disappear. This always cracked Mike up, because it reminded him of a Sponge Bob episode. And so, Harry just disappeared one day.

After the trouble with Harry, Mike would have to proceed slowly with Greg and feel out his financial issues as well as his moral compass. Greg had been kind of a bad ass in high school, taking liberties with the girls and stealing liquor from the corner Buy Rite. He got in his fair share of trouble but one way or another he always seemed to get out of it. When Greg had asked him to help with his business, Mike and Eddie did their research into Greg's background.

Mike wondered if Greg learned some shady lessons while at Lehigh. Although they found out since high school, he was as clean as a whistle. Not so much as a parking ticket or a boil on his ass. Mike, on the other hand, went to Haverford which was a strange college; he thought its students were very quirky and nerdy. Mike regretted going there because he found the food abominable, the girls not to his liking and the school mascot was a black squirrel for God's sake. But his father had been adamant because he had attended in the sixties and wanted his son to follow in his footsteps. The only good thing that came out of his schooling was hooking up with some of the other sick motherfuckers that went there. Where there is weird, there is also devious, twisted and genius. All he had to do was go drinking or get high with some of these guys and they would start talking shit. They would tell him about these wild financial schemes they were planning, from Ponzi schemes to money laundering ideas to internet fraud. All these ideas led him to his current plan to increase his wealth. Until he learned otherwise, Mike would have to operate covertly behind Greg's back as he did with Harry.

Having access to the information on a leasing application opened up numerous possibilities for Mike to increase his cash flow. He had bank account information, name, address, phone, next of kin (sometimes), Social Security number, date of birth, work information, and previous addresses.

On top of that, many of the tenants in the Somerville area were undocumented immigrants working in the various restaurants, landscaping and construction businesses. They gained access to apartments only through a relative or friend who was a citizen or had a green card. They dealt solely in cash because without a Social Security number, they were unable to get a checking account or driver's license. If their employer paid them by personal check, they had to use a check cashing service that took a cut of their money. Many were desperate to earn extra cash just to pay for the necessities of food, clothing, shelter and transportation. The only means of transportation for some was riding a bicycle many miles to work. Mike had seen them in the rain, snow, and dark of night. He didn't see their hardship; he only saw opportunity for himself. People who were desperate to earn money to support themselves or families were willing to do anything.

Mike walked into the boiler room setup where his people were using high pressure techniques and overheard one of the men speaking in Spanish and English. "Buenos Dias, Mr. Lopez. My name is Agent Martinez, and I am with the Internal Revenue Service. It has come to our attention that you are getting paid under the table from your employer. Do you know what that means? It means that the United States Government is not receiving the taxes that should be coming out of your paycheck. It also means that other governmental functions, like the police and fire department that operate on local taxes, aren't getting their fair share from you. There are two things that can happen. Since not paying taxes is a federal crime, we can arrest and put you in prison or deport you. Or you can pay the fine. What would you like to do?"

Nine times out of ten, the person on the other end said they would pay the fine.

The conversation continued on in this way, "Since you do not have a checking account or credit card, I am afraid the only alternative would be to have you pay the fine by gift card. You will need to go to Target and buy a fifty dollar gift card by Friday. You will call me at this number and read off the serial number and activation code. You will do this every month to pay your fine and taxes.

Once his employees got the store card information, be it from Target, Walmart, ShopRite, or Bed Bath and Beyond, they would pass it on to Mike who would load it to his store app. Then he would go to the store and buy other types of gift cards. So that no one would be suspicious or link his face with the purchases, he would go to the self-checkout counters. Mike or Eddie had to convert the cards quickly so the victims couldn't access the funds cutting him off from the money. He had learned that the hard way. One of the first times he tried this scam, the victim got wise to what was happening and spent all the money on the card before Mike could convert it.

So now, the cards had to be mailed to a post office box and converted immediately. After taking possession, the card would be photographed then discarded. Mike would then sell the codes online at a discounted rate. There was no direct link to the victim.

Recently, he found he could also take advantage of people when they were in a hurry to secure an apartment, if their old lease was up, or they needed to get out of the lease for whatever reason. Some might be relocating and only had a few weeks to get an apartment lined up.

Occasionally, he was able to get money from a tenant for an apartment that he did not even own or did not really exist. He would instruct them to send a deposit to a post office box to secure the apartment otherwise it would be rented to someone else. This worked well for illegals; he would tell them this was how it was done, and they believed him. He would get the money and never show up to the meeting to hand over the keys to the apartment. This was the best because it was done over a burner phone and the prospective tenant never saw his face.

When he obtained a large list of prospective tenants, he would ask for fees to cover background checks, usually around seventy-five to one hundred dollars. He wouldn't bother to conduct the work and just pocketed all the money.

Once he secured pictures of Greg's various apartments buildings he would funnel some tenants to him, while taking advantage of the rest, the more gullible of the group. He would post pictures of the apartments on Facebook, Craig's List and various rental sites on the internet and when people called him, he would tell them that he was out of the country and that the tenant would just have to rent the unit without seeing it first or at least to send him a deposit so the apartment could be held until one of the owner's representatives could get there to finalize the lease and let the renter into the apartment. And, oh by the way, there are twenty other people interested in the apartment so the money should be sent immediately.

One of his best money makers was showing potential apartments in a foreclosed building. He would break in a few weeks in advance, change the locks, make repairs and decorate one unit, then show the potential renters that unit. He would collect the fees, deposit and first month rent then disappear. He had even seen some of these people attempt to move in, much to their dismay. Suckers!

Recently, he added credit score referrals to his money maker scheme. After a potential tenant responded by email to one of his apartment listings posted on Craigslist, he would ask for information on how long the person had been with their current employer, yearly income and credit score. He specified that the credit score be within a certain range of time. If they needed a current score, they could obtain one by using the link provided. With a current score, he would set up a viewing for the apartment. When the person clicked on the link, it would inform them that a report would be provided for a fee. Mike would get the fee and the tenant would never see the apartment.

Wire transfer services to an offshore numbered account and Western Union were his friends. Defrauded people can't come after him if they can't find him.

Mike pondered what service he would use with Greg, who was smart. He realized he needed to start out with a legitimate method. He had been thinking of a new scheme and was convinced it would work. He would begin posting apartments for rent at a great rate at the Social Security Office and the Unemployment Office. He would work through all his other money making options and the ones that fell through would be referred for Greg's real apartments. He would actually show the apartments, collect the true fees, deposits and first month rent. The kicker would be to sign these people up for direct deposit of rental checks. The Social Security check, Unemployment or Worker's Compensation check would be sent directly to the account he set up. The first month's rent, he would tell them, would have to come directly from Social Security Administration,

Worker's Compensation insurance carrier or the Unemployment Office. After that, it would need to go into a bank account and then the monthly rent would be automatically transferred on a specific date. He would have to get the exact routing numbers and banking information from that first deposit. Then things could begin to happen. Heart attacks, disappearances, hit by a car, whatever. The longer the person appeared to be alive the better. If they died, the money would dry up as soon as the agencies were notified by the police or relative. The best solution was to create a reason why the person disappeared or left, and then he could transfer their accounts to one of his offshore banks. So, his plan would be to select those people with no next of kin and continue to have their money transferred to a secured, untraceable account that only he could access. He would terminate the lease and all the utilities, notify Greg, then bring in another tenant. Greg would never have to know. He would just be interested in his high occupancy rates.

CHAPTER 6

Summer 2018

Celia, thinking back to that first kiss, realized that was when the whole affair started. They were constantly together at work attending to tenants or issues at the various apartments. He began to pick her up at her apartment in Basking Ridge, saying it was just more prudent to use one car to visit various sites and he would naturally bring her home. Sometimes, he would suggest they eat dinner at her place, and he would mysteriously find a bottle of wine in the back seat of his car, saying something corny like, "Oh look! Someone must have left this in my car. Can't let it go to waste now, can we?" Then he started to stay over. It just seemed like a natural fit. They worked well together in the business and in her bed.

As time went on, Greg began to rely on her more, increasing her responsibilities with all his properties. She oversaw everything from hiring the maintenance people for inside work, to the landscapers for outside work. Greg even suggested she move out of her apartment in Basking Ridge and live onsite at the newest property in Somerville so that she could also manage the tenant complaints and issue work orders for the staff. More importantly, it was centrally located to his other properties.

He had given her a beautiful two-bedroom apartment on the main floor near the rental office. This place was so much nicer than her old apartment and there was more room for when Kim came home from college. It also saved her money which allowed her to give her daughter a little extra spending money while she was away at school in Tampa. She would have to make sure she reported this business perk on her taxes.

Greg had approached her in the office several months ago and told her about a service he had started to use at some of his other properties just about the time she came on board. He had wanted to try it out on a small scale before rolling it out to all his properties. He hoped it would make their job a bit easier. Instead of relying on the ads placed in the newspaper and using some of the expensive marketing products, he had entered into a contract with a new company that would provide them with vetted leads for tenants. Once they cleared their screening process and signed the lease, all rent payments would be paid through an automatic transfer of funds from the tenants' bank account to theirs. Many of these new tenants were older and on Social Security, so their 'retirement' checks would be deposited into their account then the funds would transfer to the apartment account to pay their rent. They could even have the Social Security check direct deposited from the SSA. Stiff penalties were imposed on the tenant for insufficient funds in their account, but the amenities made it worth their while.

He told her the process worked great; he had been using it for a while at some of his other buildings and the tenants seemed to like it. Now that he was sure it was cost effective and a time saver, he wanted to implement the program across the board. All new tenants would be offered the service as they signed up and existing tenants could now take advantage of the direct deposit if they wanted to switch. Celia wouldn't have to be constantly calling or emailing tenants reminding them that their rent was due, and would be able to effectively manage the maintenance, landscaping and any complaints that came to her attention. She wouldn't have to make bank runs to deposit checks once they were able to get the remaining tenants on the new system. Checks would be directly deposited into their business account which Greg reconciled monthly and turned over to his buddy Fred Russo, who oversaw the accounting for all of his properties.

She agreed and soon was able to have a majority of the tenants sign up for direct deposit. Things seemed to be running smoothly. But then things changed. She began to notice odd numbers in the accounting reports and some of the tenant rumblings were a bit bizarre. It was late last spring when she heard complaints from some of their tenants about phone calls they received from the IRS. A few even had the feeling that someone had been in their apartments. When she questioned them further, they told her they thought the phone calls were scams because they paid their taxes on time and it was probably just the maintenance man coming in for the monthly pest control. Nothing was ever missing, so they never filed a formal complaint. It was just extremely odd.

CHAPTER 7

End of Summer 2018

Allister Foley had just moved into his new apartment. Living so close to the downtown area of Somerville would be very exciting. Being retired and widowed, he wanted to be able to walk to the grocery store, restaurants, shops and church and his new place was ideal for this. It was also on a bus line which was great for when his friends came to visit from New York or Newark and who did not own a car.

The apartment advertisement was posted on the bulletin board by the entrance to the Social Security Office in Bridgewater. He had just turned sixty-seven and wanted to begin the process of receiving his retirement benefits. After years of hard work, the prospect of those monthly payments along with his Teamsters' pension would be grand.

When his wife of forty-five years passed away, he felt he couldn't continue to live in his big house. Even when she was alive, it just seemed too big for the two of them. So, he listed it with a local real estate agent after making some repairs and sprucing up the paint. It sold quickly for asking price, much to his delight.

Allister had always managed his money well, and so the proceeds of the sale went into his investment account. He was quite thrilled with how his financial advisor had invested in great companies with high dividend returns. Along with the Social Security benefits, he would have a healthy, monthly income flow that would allow him to live comfortably. He couldn't wait to email his friend, Roger Newman, and show him around Somerville when he returned from England.

He had gone directly to the apartment complex, bypassing the phone call to set up an appointment. The leasing agent at the apartment complex, Celia, had been very helpful and efficient in finalizing the lease arrangements. She had even gotten the maintenance men to help him move his couch and bedroom set into his apartment. He had sold most of the furnishings in his home through an estate sale, carefully picking what he wanted to take with him in this new phase of his life. It would be hard, he missed his wife terribly, but there was nothing he could do but move on and forward.

He signed a twelve-month lease, arranged for internet service with Fios, electricity, water and gas with the local utility companies. Already possessing an iPhone, Allister splurged and bought a new Hewitt Packard laptop. He thought he might even try out Facebook and one of the online dating sites. Of course, he would get Netflix and save a ton of money by avoiding cable. Roger kept telling him it was time to get on with his life, maybe the time was now.

Celia had called him the other day and offered a new service they were setting up with the assistance of another company, O'Ryan Realty Placement Services. This company would assist him in setting up a direct deposit of his Social Security benefits or one of his other accounts, to pay his rent directly, saving him time and a stamp. Being old school and not too computer savvy, he thanked her and said he preferred the old-fashioned way of writing a check. He was pleased she didn't try to high pressure him into doing this. He liked the feeling of being in control of his finances, being the one to actually write and deliver the rent payment. There were too many stories of internet fraud, and he was worried something would go wrong. His AARP magazine had numerous articles about identity theft and hackers. Plus, it gave him something to do. There were so many empty hours in the day since his wife died and he was constantly looking for activities and outside stimulation. He hated just sitting around watching TV all day.

The next day, Allister got up early and made breakfast. Sitting at his breakfast counter drinking coffee and eating a plate of eggs and toast, he decided to send his friend Roger an email. He had been sending him a note about every week or so, keeping his friend updated on his activities.

He began telling him more about selling his house, seeing the apartment ad, beginning his Social Security, moving and the various services and benefits of living in his new apartment. He went on to say how much he missed his wife but with Roger's help, he hoped that he could begin to live again. He asked Roger to come visit as soon as he returned to the States. Before he could hit send, there was a knock at the door. He didn't want to take the chance of losing the almost complete email before he was done, so he saved it as a draft. He had learned the hard way after writing a long email, hitting the wrong key and watching everything disappear. Then, without thinking, he re-entered Roger's email address in a new document and cut and pasted the original message in the new email. He really didn't understand the process, so he tended to take unnecessary steps.

He got up from the counter, went to the door and looked through the peep hole saying, "Who's there?"

"Mr. Foley, my name is Mike, and I am from O'Ryan Realty Placement Services. I was wondering if I could come in and discuss our services with you."

"Thank you, but Celia already told me about the services, and I am not interested," Allister said without opening the door.

Mike, not one to be told no, said, "Mr. Foley, I understand how confusing our process might be, but it is secure, and we even offer two hundred dollars off one month's rent if you sign up."

This got Allister's attention and he opened the door and asked Mike to come in. Just before he closed the door another man came in quickly. Mike introduced him as Eddie, his technology specialist.

Allister didn't know too much about technology experts, but he did know thugs. In his working years, Allister was a Teamster, driving big rigs around the United States hauling anything that would give him a good paycheck. Eddie was tall, with a thick neck, large biceps and hands that looked like hams. He had seen his type too many times and wasn't sure those hands could type on a keyboard without hitting multiple keys at once.

Allister backed away from the door as Eddie shut it. Contemplating what he should do, he thought he should at least get his phone in his hand should it be needed to call for help.

Mike saw the fear on Allister's face and tried to alleviate it.

"Mr. Foley don't be frightened. Eddie is rough around the edges but believe me, he is only here to help. Why don't we sit down, and I'll give you more details about our services?"

Allister wasn't having any of Mike's bullshit. He knew intimidation when he saw it. He grabbed his phone and tried to punch in 911, but Eddie was fast as well as large. He grabbed Allister's hand and squeezed it until Allister dropped the phone.

"Mr. Foley, now please sit down and keep your mouth shut. I pride myself on having a high compliance rate with my program. It upsets me that you seem to distrust me and my associate."

As Mike was talking, Eddie began to carefully look around the apartment, gathering various documents from Allister's desk, bedroom and wallet. He then went to the laptop, opened it to the letter Allister had been typing to his friend Roger and began to write.

"Hey, what are you doing?" screamed Allister. Mike immediately jumped up and grabbed Allister's arm and painfully twisted it behind him.

"I suggest you not yell and when asked, provide the information we want or you will have permanent damage," hissed Mike.

Whimpering, Allister said, "What is it that you want from me?"

"We want the passwords to all of your accounts: Social Security, pension, utilities, email and banking. Eddie, does he have credit cards in the wallet?"

"Yeah, he does."

"We also want the credit card passwords, too. If you would have just signed up like Celia suggested, you could have avoided all this. Now, write down all passwords, account numbers and sign this form."

Allister was finding it hard to think of a way out of this situation. What would they do to him if he didn't give them what they wanted, worse yet what would they do to him if he did? He decided he didn't have a choice; he was sure he was going to die either way so he would give them the information. If they killed him, then maybe the police could trace their transactions and arrest them. If he didn't, they would probably kill him anyway and would leave with nothing and there would be no tracks to follow.

Picking up the pen and paper, Allister slowly began to list all the accounts and passwords.

As he did so, Eddie checked to make sure they could access each account. Allister had yet to sign the document that gave O'Ryan Realty Placement Services authority to request direct deposit of Allister's Social Security monthly payments. Mike called Eddie over in hopes of influencing him. Eddie grabbed his hand and began to squeeze it. The pain was unbearable, and he relinquished, signing the paper the best he could. It felt like all the bones had been broken in his hand.

He felt so defeated, knowing they wouldn't let him live after he gave them all his information. He desperately tried to think of a way to leave a clue about his killers' identities. Then Eddie came up behind him.

CHAPTER 8

Eddie had edited Allister's email and sent it to Roger saying he had moved into his new apartment, giving the address, but wasn't sure he could stay alone. With his wife's passing he felt so alone and didn't know if he could go on. And just yesterday, he fell in the shower, hurting his hand. He hoped Roger would understand how depressed he felt and not judge him.

What Eddie and Mike didn't know was that Roger had returned from London, received the disturbing email and was on his way over to see Allister. Fearing Allister was going to kill himself, he rushed to the new apartment hoping to get there before Allister did something stupid.

Knowing he had little time now they had his financial information and passwords, Allister did his best to slip out of Eddie's grip and was able to run into his bedroom. In a futile attempt to lock his door, he put his whole-body weight against it, but Eddie was too big and too strong. Allister fell to the floor and was struggling to get up when Eddie took a pillow from the bed and fell on top of him. With the air knocked out of his lungs, Allister knew he was doomed. The pillow was pushed against his nose and mouth, he silently said his last prayer and hoped his wife would be welcoming him to Heaven.

As soon as Mike entered the bedroom to help Eddie with Allister's body, they heard the door to the apartment open and someone was calling out Allister's name. Startled, Mike grabbed the laptop and Eddie picked up the cell phone. Looking around the small room, they quickly decided the best course of action was to hide in the walk-in closet. Neither wanted to deal with a second body and hopefully whoever it was wouldn't start snooping around when they found Allister's body. They knew there was no phone in the apartment because they had it with them in the closet. The man would have to use his own. If need be, they would knock him out before he could call the police and silently slip away.

"Oh, God Allister! What have you done? Oh, shit, where is your phone?" They heard him leave the apartment, presumably to call for help.

Quickly, Mike and Eddie grabbed Allister by the arms and legs and carried him out of the apartment. They had the foresight to not drag him, this way it would look like he wasn't dead and left of his own volition. The last thing they needed was evidence that two feet were dragged across the bedroom carpet leaving a trail right out the front door.

There was a second set of stairs on the other side of the apartment leading to the back parking lot that only tenants were aware of. Mike had parked his van there, and they loaded Allister's body in the back. No one was around to see them load the corpse and drive away.

CHAPTER 9

"Shit, shit, shit" Mike said pounding his hand on the steering wheel of the van as they quickly exited the parking lot. "That is NOT how I wanted that to go! I wanted him to play nice. I should have left you behind, you scared the shit out of him. I am positive I could have talked him into the direct deposit of his rent. But no, you and your freakish size. Do you know who you remind me of? The Creeper, that guy in the Sherlock Holmes movie, I think it was the *Pearl of Death*. He was huge and frightening, just like you. You are going to have to stay in the background going forward. Now what am I going to do with him?"

"Hey, Mikey, don't sweat it! The guy that came in won't know what happened. We left no trace; we have the accounts and passwords, and we have the body that we can get rid of. They will think Allister was alive and walked away. With his email information I can send his buddy another note leading him on a wild goose chase. Plus, I got a look at our guy's accounts when I was making sure we had access and he is loaded!"

"Eddie, our first priority is to dispose of this body, so no one EVER finds it. Maybe you can go out of state to Pennsylvania and buy a bunch of lye and find a nice safe place to rot him away, you know like what you do with a dead deer carcass that ends up on your lawn and no one will take it away. While you are doing that, I will deal with the accounts and email."

"Na, I got a better idea," said Eddie. "I gotta buddy in Maryland that runs a funeral parlor. He does alkaline hydrolysis where they get rid of bodies kinda like cremation but without the fire. They put the body in a big tank with a lye solution and circulating water heated to about three hundred degrees and cook 'em down for six to eight hours with a little pressure. Kinda like a stew in a pressure cooker. What's left? No DNA, no RNA, just a coffee like solution. He can be flushed down the sink or toilet. EPA friendly remains. No sweat. May cost us, but I'll see what kinda deal I can work out. I still have Harry stored in the freezer in my garage. Maybe he will give us a two for one deal."

Mike drove the van to his house, gave the keys to Eddie and told him not to come back until the job was done. He took the phone, laptop and papers inside. After he made himself a big martini, he sat down at his desk to begin what would be a long night's work.

By five the next morning, Mike, in Allister's name, had transferred funds, closed accounts and cancelled utilities and phone. He thought and thought about an explanation for Allister's disappearance. Deciding two emails were needed right away, he wrote an email to Allister's friend apologizing for running away. He also sent an email to Celia Ravenscroft informing her that he was vacating the property. The email explained how embarrassed and unhappy he was and promised to be in touch as soon as he found a better place to live. He hadn't been happy there and knew he had to make a quick, clean break. Mike figured he had a day or two until he would need to transfer the accounts to another location. He moved his funds on a regular basis hoping to make it difficult to track him down. It would give him time to think and plan. Eddie was becoming a liability. He had told him to take care of Harry after he became suspicious of the two of them. Now with another dead body on their hands, Eddie would surely hit him up for more than his usual salary.

CHAPTER 10

Week after Labor Day 2018

It had been a week since Roger Newman reported seeing Allister dead on his bedroom floor. There had been no news from the police or Roger.

As her usual Monday morning routine, Celia put on a pot of coffee, retrieved mail from the mailbox from the Saturday afternoon delivery and reviewed and noted all voicemails left by tenants and prospective renters. Her next agenda item was to log into the computer and check emails. That's where she found an email from the tenant that she had thought was dead. She read through it once, and then re-read it again. Apparently, he had not been happy there and decided to vacate his apartment. She wondered if he realized that by doing so, he would lose his security deposit and still be responsible for the remaining months of rent on his lease, which would be a sizeable chunk of change. And what about his furniture and belongings that he left? Shaking her head in disbelief she called Miranda to tell her the news.

"Miranda? Hi, this is Celia. You aren't going to believe this, but I just got an email from our dead tenant. He says he didn't like it here and left. Between you and me, I find this strange because he was such a nice guy and seemed to be thrilled to live here. I guess now that we have something in writing we can clean out his apartment and begin the rental process. I just wanted to let you know that I will be calling O'Ryan to have them send a referral."

Miranda sat and listened as Celia told her about Allister rising from the grave. She asked, "Did you call his friend Roger Newman and tell him?"

"No, I called you first. Do you think I should?" asked Celia.

"Yes, I think it would be a good idea and see if he has heard from Allister. If there is any damage to the apartment, or he owes any money, we will need to know where to find him. I don't want to lose any money on this. You can try responding to the email and tell him he stills owes rent for the remainder of his lease."

As soon as Celia disconnected with Miranda, she looked up Roger Newman's number in her file on Allister and placed the call. The phone was answered immediately.

"Mr. Newman, this Celia Ravenscroft. I am the property manager where your friend Allister Foley lived. I just wanted to let you know I received an email from him this morning. Have you heard from him?"

"Yes, I have. What did your email say?" he anxiously asked.

"He said he wasn't happy here and decided to leave. I have checked and all of his utilities and services have been disconnected, which would require an account and password to complete, so that leads me to believe he is still alive."

"Ms. Ravenscroft, I find this so bizarre. Allister was not the kind of person to make quick, rash decisions. It took him almost a year to just decide to sell his house after his wife died. He hated change. He was barely in this apartment, and he moves out leaving all his things and forfeiting his deposits? And there is another thing that signals to me that something is off. He signed his email to me 'Al.' In the past, it was always Allister. By the way, did you find his computer that he wrote the email on? I am almost certain he had a computer, laptop or iPad. And if I remember correctly, when someone sends an email from their phone, at the end of the email it says, 'Sent From My iPhone.' It seems strange that he wrote me minutes before I got there, and we couldn't find his computer. Would the police have taken it? Or did he take it with him? I am not sure what is going on, but whatever it is, it is not good. If you hear any more from him or receive any mail or packages, I would appreciate it if you would let me know."

"Of course," agreed Celia. "I agree this is beginning to bother me too. I plan on contacting the police to let them know about my email from him and ask about the computer. Let me know if you hear anything also. He still owes his rent money for the remainder of the lease." With that, Celia hung up the phone and debated calling Miranda back. Nothing was for certain, and she didn't want to speculate without more facts. She decided to wait until after she phoned the police about Allister's computer and having received an email from the man.

CHAPTER 11

Roger kept thinking about the original and subsequent emails from Allister. 'Your friend, Al.' He never called himself just Al, thought Roger. Something is just not right.

Sitting there at his desk in his home, with the email in front of him, he wondered under what conditions would Allister call himself Al?

Maybe he had a new girlfriend and she preferred to call him Al, so he adopted the moniker.

Maybe he was under duress, and he signed it Al hoping Roger would get the hint something was amiss.

Maybe he was typing but was interrupted and hadn't finished typing his full name. But would that have happened twice? Roger was sure Allister would have proofread his letter before sending it and having found the error, would correct it.

When Roger was in the apartment with the police filling out the missing person report, they had searched the apartment for the missing devices and found neither.

Where was he? Where were the devices? And why hadn't Allister responded to his emails and phone calls?

Looking again at the email, Roger had an idea. Allister's email account was AFoley@aol.com. If he could figure out Allister's AOL password, maybe he could find some hints about where Allister might have gone.

Would he only have a few attempts at cracking the password code until AOL shut him down? He would have to come up with three strong possible passwords before even trying. If he failed, it would be up to the police to hack into the account.

He thought for a while and decided the password probably included Allister's late wife's name. Then, it could be her birthdate, their wedding date, the date they met or the date she died.

Roger entered the username then tried the wife's birthdate. No good. Next, he tried their wedding date. That didn't work either. He was almost certain he had only one more attempt before getting locked out. He remembered another friend whose wife died. He had had that date tattooed on his wrist. Roger knew how strong Allister's love was for his wife, so he entered her date of death and was relieved when he gained access to Allister's email account.

He began to search through and read all incoming and sent emails. He checked spam and trash mail. Not seeing anything that would give him a hint as to what happened to Allister he was about to close out of the account and let it go. Then he saw the link for drafts and the number one after it. He clicked on it and opened a letter addressed to Roger written on the date and at the approximate time of his disappearance.

As he was reading the email, his heartbeat began to accelerate, and he began to have trouble breathing. This proved something bad had happened to Allister. He immediately thought 'I have to call Celia Ravenscroft and the police.'

Miranda received a phone call from Tim Morris, the officer investigating the disappearance of Allister Foley. He asked if she and Celia Ravenscroft could meet him at the station in Somerville. Mr. Newman had contacted him stating he had vital information about Allister's disappearance and wanted everyone to meet.

Miranda arranged to pick up Celia at the apartment building. As they were driving the short distance to the station, Celia asked, "Do you have any ideas what's going on?"

"No,' said Miranda, "other than Roger said he had some evidence he wanted to share."

When they arrived at police headquarters, Detective Morris led them into a conference room; Roger was already seated with his laptop open on the table.

"I knew something wasn't right about his disappearance!" Roger blurted out impatiently. "With Allister's laptop missing and having received a number of emails but no phone calls, I couldn't understand why he said what he did in those emails and had signed it 'Al.' He never did that in the past."

Roger swiveled his laptop screen around to face Miranda, Celia and Detective Morris. An AOL email screen was visible, and a letter addressed to Roger dated the day Allister disappeared. The group read the letter, looked at the time of the draft, then looked at each other.

Detective Morris was the first to speak. "Mr. Newman, how did you find this? Was it sent to you?"

"No, I knew Allister had AOL as his email provider and guessed at his password. I found this letter in his drafts. The others that we received are in his sent email section. You can see they are clearly different and are totally opposite in meaning. And another thing, look how he signed the draft 'Al,' then look at all the other emails he had written, they are all signed 'Allister.'

Miranda who had been deep in thought suddenly sat up and said, "It's almost like he was writing you a letter telling you how great everything was in his new apartment and was interrupted before he could finish the signature and send it to you. Maybe someone came to the door, and he saved it to draft to finish up after whoever left. But then, why the reversal in the tone of the email? And where is he, his phone and his laptop?"

Detective Morris stood, collecting the notes he had been taking and said, "With this strange twist and his email password, I am going to have our tech guys do some digging, and see if we can trace some of his financial activities to locate him. Maybe he has used a credit card, debit card, checked into a hotel or rented a car. We will start questioning the neighbors at the apartment to see if anyone remembers seeing anything the day he disappeared. Does anyone else have anything?" asked Detective Morris.

Celia showed the email she had received, giving the detective a copy.

"Thank you all for coming in. Please let me know immediately if you receive anything else or hear from Mr. Foley. I, too, find it very odd and disturbing that he has not called you directly Mr. Newman."

"Me, too" said Roger sadly.

Keslie Patch-Bohrod

CHAPTER 12

End of September 2018

A few weeks later over breakfast, Greg was pouring Celia a cup of coffee, "I forgot to tell you yesterday while we were in the Raritan complex, that there is a new vacancy. I don't have much time today, otherwise I would take care of it, so could you do me a favor and contact Mike and ask him to fill it for us?"

Curious, she asked him about the circumstances of the vacancy.

"Oh, he was an elderly man," began Greg. "His kids had gone to visit him and found his door open, and he was gone. They presumed he wandered off. The police are still looking for him; they put out a Silver Alert. It happens all the time. His kids plan to put him in a memory impaired assisted living facility as soon as they find him. They have removed his stuff and paid all the rent due, so you can get it cleaned and ready for rental as soon as possible."

Celia said she would get on it right away. But then she stopped, sat down and began to think about it. If he had dementia, why would he have been left alone in an apartment, especially the one in Raritan that was in a high traffic area? Maybe his kids didn't know that he was losing his mental capacity. She knew some people didn't maintain regular contact with their parents or maybe the kids lived out of state and hadn't seen him in a while. Something wasn't right. Is this a coincidence? Two strange events so close together.

CHAPTER 13

Sunday, September 30, 2018

Fall was always bittersweet for Miranda. The kids off to college, returning home from a summer on Long Beach Island, her Loveladies Ennui on hold until next May. This year was a bit tougher with Kevin away in London participating in a finance internship. Happily, he was doing well, and not missing home. Miranda, however, was missing him. She and Jack saw Erica most weekends when she had a home field hockey game at her college. But with Kevin so far away, she didn't know if she could stand it until December when the program ended, and he would return home.

Thankfully, she and Jack had plenty of activities to keep them busy for the next few months: getting acquainted with running an apartment building, Chowderfest at the shore, Napa vacation and finally her cousin's wedding at Thanksgiving in South Carolina.

Miranda knew she would be exhausted come Christmas time, but she desperately needed the distraction to keep her mind from drifting back to the events of the summer. She still couldn't believe there had been a Soviet spy living so close to them.

She had looked forward to a quiet summer filled with family, rest and tasty food. Instead, it was filled with dread, death and depression. Now these issues at the apartment were cropping up.

Maybe they would spend the kids' winter vacation at the shore this year. It would be extremely cold and desolate on the lagoon, but the thought of turning up the heat, wrapping up in a blanket with their dog Maynard snuggling beside her would be pure deliciousness. There would be nothing to do other than read, talk, watch television and cook. After all their studying, she was sure the kids would enjoy that, maybe even inviting some of their friends down.

Each October, Long Beach Island, New Jersey held a Chowderfest in Beach Haven where local restaurants would vie for the title of best chowder. Miranda and Jack had gone numerous times over the years and always looked forward to the many different variations of Manhattan and New England clam chowder the chefs could concoct. There would be music, craft beers, wine and tons of people.

This year, the Chowderfest was being held the end of September. This was an extremely popular event, and more and more people were coming onto the island to partake in the festivities. The Craig's plan was to take the LBI Shuttle on Sunday from their Loveladies home to the event saving time, money and aggravation by not having to find or pay for parking. Plus, they knew they would try at least three or four of the different local IPA beers (or maybe more depending on how good they were) during the day and wouldn't want to risk a DUI trying to drive themselves back to their shore house on the other end of the island.

Miranda was looking forward to returning to Long Beach Island, knowing things would be back to normal after the threats had been alleviated.

The sign announcing the festivities greeted the Craigs on the right side of the roadway as they were making their way off the bridge to Long Beach Island. The activities began on September twenty-ninth with the Merchant Mart. The Chowder Cook-Off Classic would be held the next day on September thirtieth at Taylor Avenue Ball Field in Beach Haven. The event always took place the weekend before Columbus Day and brought in several million dollars in revenues each year to the local businesses. Jack and Miranda always tried to participate to show their support for the island community, although they usually only went to the cook-off on Sunday. This was the thirtieth year the event had taken place and the weather looked like it was going to be glorious. She recalled the one year that it had rained, but thankfully stopped in time for the festivities to begin. Miranda and Jack quickly unloaded their car and got Maynard, their Weimaraner Chocolate Labrador mix, fed and situated at their shore house. The end of September was always beautiful, sometimes better than during the summer. The crowds were down, the temperature was perfect, water conditions on the bay were ideal and ennui was just a sunset away.

After feeding Maynard, Miranda and Jack went to the backyard with their dog, surveying their domain. It was almost melancholy, the feeling that swept through them.

"Jack, just looking around at the houses on our lagoon, I find it hard to imagine what it was like during the 1950s and 1960s during Silvermaster and Ullmann times; and for that matter, during the times when Chicky, Alek and Frederick started coming here during their summers. Their cohorts were so original, so different yet everyone was accepting. Imagine, people accepted Silvermaster and Ullmann even though they were accused Soviet spies. Maybe it was because there was a group of communist thinking people here that welcomed the camaraderie that their notoriety implied. I remember your father telling stories of the communists, beatniks, gay people, Jews and the artsy fartsy types, his words not mine. Visualize a group of people gathered like that now with all the anti-Semitic, homophobic, liberals and right wingers? Everyone trying to change how the other believed when they only wanted to believe in themselves. "

"What makes me saddest of all was the look on Frederick's face when he entered our backyard party over the summer, and it was filled with neighbors. It showed shock, sadness and fear. He did not know anyone except us and Liz. Everything he had known was gone, the houses were all changed, the people and their ideals had changed, probably for the worst, and he felt he was left with nothing. He would have been a total outsider had it not been for Liz rescuing him and directing the conversation toward something he was comfortable with- the past."

"We are lucky in that we have developed friendships with most of our neighbors. There are people on our street who do not venture out or only have their group of friends or relatives who don't live on the island. How lonely that must be; how lonely that will be in the future if they continue to live down here. I know how I feel when I come down here in the winter and no one is around. I guess that is how they might feel. Maybe they want the friendships but just don't know how to go about it."

"You know, I think men have an easier time of it. They can go out on their own, sit at a bar, order some food and strike up a conversation. If a woman goes out on her own, she immediately gets labeled as "looking" or some other sad term. So, what does she do? She stays at home by herself. Maybe her husband has to work and will be coming down on the weekend. If no one is around, she won't go out and try to strike up a conversation in a bar because firstly, there won't be other single women there. There will be men there or couples and they will think she is out looking for fun and sex, which would not be safe. I wish someone would come up with an idea to create a mechanism for women on the island to meet women like themselves, who want to meet for a drink or dinner and safe conversation and fun. Just think of what a network like that would do for women's self-esteem."

"God, Miranda. What the hell brought that on?" asked Jack.

"Oh, I don't know. Just reflecting, I guess. Like what's with Allister Foley's disappearance?

If he left on purpose, he doesn't give a rat's ass for all the trouble he's causing and the torment his best friend is experiencing. If someone else is responsible, then it's an even bigger problem."

"I'm just getting so sick and tired of what I see going on. The disrespect, lying, disregard for others. It just seems to get worse by the day. We have seen this decline over the years, but it seems to be escalating. It's not just the haves versus the have nots, it's the haves that want more and their 'damn you' attitude. When you call out bad behavior, they turn it against you, spin it to make it your fault. I just won't take it anymore. This summer showed me I have to take a stand. You must take a stand. We all do for what is right, legal and moral. Remember how angry I was when our "friends" drove over our planting bed in our driveway and didn't tell us or bother to fix it? And how, when I found out, another friend said, 'I don't want to get involved, I don't want to ruin my friendship with either of you?' That's cowardice and wrong. It's like if someone accused me of a heinous crime that was impossible for me to commit and our 'friends' replied in the same manner not wanting to offend the accuser even though they knew it was ludicrous."

The two were silent as they walked to the end of their street, checked the LBI Shuttle app on their iPhone and saw that their ride would be at their street in a few minutes.

As Miranda and Jack jumped on the van to make their way to the ball field, their bus driver told them that rumor had it there were over thirteen thousand people attending, based on the number of tickets sold so far. They marveled how the event had grown in popularity over the years.

Once they got near the festival, they asked the driver to drop them on the boulevard across the street from the B&B Department store. They would walk down the side street to the entrance gate. Large, white tents had been put up to house all the table stations. There were stations for drinks and plenty of porta johns. Miranda noticed an increase in security with large police vehicles parked strategically around the event to preclude any vehicle from making its way into the crowds. Backpacks and bags were prohibited, along with a number of other safety measures being put in place. Miranda knew first-hand about the dangers that lurked on the island from her run-in that summer with a Russian spy and the murders. It was a shame their world had come to this and just reinforced her earlier rant.

Enjoying their beer and chowder tastings, Miranda and Jack ambled through the crowds. It took time to make their way to each restaurant's table, get their little plastic cup of chowder and get away without spilling any. Many festival goers had what looked like a painter's palette with large holes drilled across the top where they placed the cups of chowder. Each time Jack and Miranda attended the Chowderfest, they vowed to get a palette for the next year. Here they were again trying to balance cups of chowder and beer without the aid of a palette. They tasted as many as possible and finally made their way to the booth to cast their votes for the best red and white chowder.

Miranda and Jack didn't stay for the closing ceremonies; they were hoping to jump onto a shuttle just prior to the announcement of the winners. They really didn't care who won, all tasted rather good to them. The crowd was starting to get the same idea and people began to congregate near the curb to wait for the next shuttle.

Later they would find out the winners were Lefty's Tavern for red, Howard's Restaurant for white and Blue Water Café for the most creative chowder. There was even a chowder ice cream, which Miranda thought was gross, but Jack being an ice cream fanatic, loved it. Overall, nineteen restaurants cooked up a storm and offered the event goers a wide variety of chowder to choose from.

Miranda's phone rang and she answered it, "Hi, this is Miranda."

"Hi Miranda, it's Celia. Boy it sounds noisy where you are."

"Celia, I can hardly hear you, there are so many people around us and we are trying to get on a shuttle bus. Is everything alright?"

"I think so, but I am noticing a few strange things."

"What did you say?" Miranda shoved her finger in the opposite ear of where the phone was held. "Did you say strange things?"

"There has been another strange disappearance."

"Celia, I can't hear you, please call me tomorrow or the next day. Jack and I are heading out to Napa, California on Wednesday for our annual wine buying trip, so I won't be in the office but will be available by phone if you need me."

"Miranda, I really need to talk to you about this, I think something is going on." Celia realized Miranda had already hung up the phone and hadn't heard her.

Getting back to their shore house after a long day of eating chowder and drinking beer, Miranda was anxious for a shower, some television and bed. She knew she should call Celia back, but she just didn't have the energy right then.

The plan had been to drive back north after breakfast on Monday, get the laundry done and begin to pack for their Wednesday flight to San Francisco. Miranda decided the best time to talk with Celia would be during the ride back home.

Once they were on the Garden State Parkway, with Jack driving, Miranda pulled her cell phone out of her purse and called Celia. She would most likely be in the office and they could have a long chat if needed.

"Hi Celia, it's Miranda. We're on our way now, I can finally hear you and you have my undivided attention."

"I'm so glad you called me back. I hardly slept last night. More and more tenants are complaining about scam phone calls and letters. Plus, Greg just told me about one of his tenants that apparently wandered off, but I'm not so sure it's that simple. I have a bad feeling something else is going on."

"Celia were the police called about Greg's tenant?" asked Miranda.

"Yes, and they are looking for him. They think he has dementia or Alzheimer's but I don't know. Why hasn't there been any other indication this man had problems?"

"Maybe the kids or his physician missed some important signs or symptoms that had just begun to appear," suggested Miranda. "Maybe he had been skilled in hiding his cognitive problems or maybe it is something completely different. "

"Oh, you are probably right. I guess I'm making a mountain out of a mole hill where a mole hill doesn't even exist" lamented Celia.

"Celia, I know you are a good person, and you really look out for each of your tenants. Honestly, right now, there is nothing you or I can do to solve these disappearances. The police are involved and will hopefully find both of them. In the meantime, all we can do is carry on and provide the police with whatever information we have. Jack and I are leaving Wednesday, so keep in touch and let me know if you hear of anything. I feel so guilty leaving you alone to deal with this, but really there is nothing you can do."

Miranda hung up the phone and turned to Jack. "Well, things are getting weird; Celia said another tenant has gone missing. It's one of Greg's, not ours."

Jack thought for a moment as he passed a string of slow-moving cars in the center lane, "It sounds like a coincidence, different apartment complexes, and different cities. I'm sure if we looked at the statistics of these cities, we would find a bunch of people who go missing on a weekly basis. Just look at the number of Silver Alerts we have had over the last few months."

"You're probably right" agreed Miranda, "I remember two if not three."

CHAPTER 14

Maybeth had been born and raised in Alexander City, Alabama, or Alex City as everyone in those parts called it, but when she met Rex Martin, her neighbor's brother, she began to reconsider where she might eventually be buried. She always had thought of herself as a true Southern Belle and had never given a second thought about moving away from the South.

She grew up enjoying the water sports on Lake Martin. Her parents had worked for years in the textile industry and of course for Russel Manufacturing Company making all those sporting goods in the 1960s. Alex City was a great place to live, and it was so close to the big cities of Birmingham, Auburn and Montgomery, which were all about an hour away, depending on how fast you drove.

Last winter, her neighbor Nancy Conners (nee Martin), invited her over for a dinner party. There would be a few other neighbors joining also, but her friend was especially excited because her brother Rex would be visiting from New Jersey. Nancy and her brother grew up in Bridgewater, where he still lived. Nancy had met her husband Rob while attending Auburn University, and they were married soon after graduation. They moved to Alexander City, Alabama to start their family and had both landed jobs with the Russel Corporation, newly named in the early 1980s.

Maybeth and her husband Glenn had moved into the same neighborhood as Nancy and Rob a few years later. The couples became fast friends, spending much of their free time together until about five years ago when Glenn died as a result of an auto accident.

It had been hard on Maybeth, and she found the memories to be too much at times. But she continued to move forward with the help of her Baptist minister and dear friend Nancy.

Maybeth thought Nancy had seen the change in her. She felt like a load had suddenly lifted and she was becoming more optimistic and open to new ideas. Maybe that was why Nancy orchestrated the dinner party, knowing Maybeth was ready to start dating again at sixty-five.

Rex stayed on at his sister's house for two months. He too was a widower and ready to move on. His decision to stay longer happened after he met Maybeth at his sister's house.

In no time, they were seeing each other daily and Maybeth was not happy with the thought of Rex eventually returning to his home in Bridgewater, New Jersey.

One day he broached the subject and asked if she might consider moving to the North so they could continue to date. He wasn't sure if he was ready to re-marry, but he knew he wanted to continue to see her. He had a little furniture making business up there with many loyal customers that kept him busy during his retirement, and frankly couldn't stand the summer heat. Otherwise, he might consider moving to Alabama.

After much thought and discussion with Rex as well as Nancy, Maybeth decided to sell her house and rent an apartment near Rex. She was desperately in need of a change and could always move back and rent something if things didn't work out between the two of them. Her house was too big just for her and the thought of all the continued maintenance it would require cemented her decision.

Rex offered to help her find a suitable place with all the amenities to make her life easier. They searched various apartment websites until they found many that seemed to fit the bill. There were several units with differing availability which was perfect since she needed to sell her house first.

Things seemed to move along very quickly. Her house sold, the estate sale took care of ridding her of old furniture and possessions and an apartment was available when she was ready.

Maybeth, with the assistance of Rex, filled out the online forms and used her credit card to pay the deposit to hold the unit. She was pleased with the woman helping her, Celia Ravenscroft. Celia told her she could use their direct deposit service where her Social Security checks would be automatically transferred to pay her monthly rent, which would save her the hassle of writing and mailing her monthly check.

With everything finalized and set, Rex and Maybeth loaded up a U-Haul trailer with her remaining possessions and secured it to the trailer hitch on her car. The two would take several days to drive north, stopping to visit Nashville for a day. The plan was to visit the Grand Ole Opry to take a daytime backstage tour and the Parthenon in Centennial Park. There would not be much time to see any other landmarks because they wanted to enjoy some of the restaurants and bars with live music that highlighted up and coming country music performers. After staying the night at the DoubleTree Hotel, they would finish their drive to Somerville, New Jersey for her new start.

It had been wonderful. She bought new furniture for her apartment and added cute curtains in each room to cover over the plain horizontal blinds installed by the apartment complex. She and Rex went to dinners, movies and shows at the local theaters. There seemed to be so much to do and see, she felt a bit overwhelmed at times, but nonetheless thrilled at the prospects before her.

Maybeth would see her apartment manager, Celia, around the building almost every week and Celia would ask how she was doing. They would chat for a while and Maybeth would tell her all the wonderful things she and Rex were doing and how happy she was living there.

It was the beginning of October, when Maybeth was balancing her checkbook and reviewing her online accounts that she noticed some strange withdrawals. Her immediate thought was that this was the beginning of Alzheimer's and she had removed money and completely forgot doing so. She thought about it and checked the dates on the activity. On her calendar, she had noted shopping and a hair appointment. She couldn't have done this. Then a horrible thought crossed her mind. How well did she really know Rex? He had not been around that day; he said he had a doctor's appointment. Could he have gotten into her handbag or her apartment and retrieved her checking information or somehow figured out her passwords? She did have them written down in a special notebook near her computer in her little office area off the bedroom. Was that why he really wanted her to move to New Jersey so he could fleece her out of her life savings?

He was the only person she knew of who came into her apartment; she always kept it locked up tight. She couldn't believe he would have the audacity to steal from her. They were actually starting to talk about getting married and buying a place together. Now? She was uncertain about her feelings toward him.

Signing onto her AOL account, Maybeth deciding to send Rex an email, not trusting herself to remember all she wanted to say to him if she did it in person. She needed to also ask him about the accounts, her moving up to Somerville to be near him. Her email to him was scathing; accusing him of all the awful things she believed him guilty of. In closing, she said she did not want to see him anymore and that she did not trust him. She hit the 'send' link and off it went.

When she returned to her mail she noticed an email alert from the Social Security Administration, notifying her that she, or someone, had changed her password.

"How dare he!" she said aloud to herself. "He's even stealing my Social Security! I had better go to the police station and file a report against him."

CHAPTER 15

Mike and Eddie had been keeping a close eye on the old lady since she moved into the apartment in Somerville. The credit check they ran on her showed a tidy sum thanks to the sale of a house in Alabama. She also had an investment account with Fidelity Investments where she kept the proceeds of her husband's wrongful death lawsuit. Of course, not willing to let even a penny get away, they tapped into her Social Security too, through the direct deposit scheme. Having all her financial data and Social Security number from her apartment lease application forms made it so easy to access any and all of her accounts.

They observed her getting really chummy with some guy and knew they had to act before she moved in with him or decided to marry him. They wouldn't be able to get their hands on her money as easily as they could now.

Soon after Maybeth had moved in, Mike and Eddie had broken into her apartment, disguised as maintenance men performing routine pest control services. They could go in every month if needed. They found her book of passwords, email, bank and investment account information and began to quickly make the transfers before she could find out. Mike and Eddie laughed at how careless and trusting people were. Tenants didn't realize how many different people have access to their apartments. Did they really think no one would look around the apartment? The elderly especially, weren't savvy in the ways of cyber-crimes and didn't put much thought to password protection.

Eddie had installed software onto her computer so he could mirror her activities whenever she signed on. He had been spending most of his time just waiting for her to log on, ever since Mike told him to quit hanging around the apartments scarring the tenants. Luckily, she was a creature of habit and would only use her computer in the mornings, freeing up Eddie's afternoon and evenings for other unsavory activities. He saw as she checked her accounts and emails and began to write a letter to her boyfriend.

Her facial expression said it all. Eddie knew she had no idea he could see her through her laptop camera lens at the top of her screen. Guess she had never heard about duct tape over the camera lens.

"Hey, Mikey, come here! I think we need to get over to Old Lady Roberts apartment right now. She knows something is wrong. It also looks like she thinks it is her boyfriend that is pilfering her stash of money."

Mike looked over Eddie's shoulder and read the email Maybeth was writing to Rex.

"This is perfect, but we have to get over there right now before she gets in touch with the police. If we can get rid of her quick, they will suspect the boyfriend when they read that email."

They jumped into the van and got to her apartment within five minutes. They located her car and were able to park right next to it on the driver's side.

"Eddie, you stay here in case she comes out and I miss her," said Mike as he exited the van. "If she is really planning on going to the police, she will come out to her car. Best you stay here just in case."

As with Allister, he used the back stairway to hopefully avoid being spotted by any of the other tenants. He knocked on her door, but no one answered. As he went down the back stairway again, he heard some car doors open, a muffled sound, then three doors closing. He ran the rest of the way to the van just as Eddie was starting it.

"She was just getting into her car, so I grabbed her, knocked her out and shoved her in the back of the van. Let's go before somebody sees us," an agitated Eddie shouted as he began to drive away.

"Eddie, drop me at my place, then take care of her like you did Allister and Harry. Your buddy was OK doing this right? Do you need any cash?" asked Mike.

"Na, I'm good. He prefers a wire transfer to his Cayman account which we can do later after the job is complete."

A few minutes later, Mike got out of the van and Eddie drove off to have Maybeth Roberts reduced to sludge.

CHAPTER 16

Eddie decided to stop off at home before making the drive to Maryland again. He needed to finish her off, then gather supplies to scrub his van after he unloaded the dead lady at the funeral home.

First, he grabbed the bleach, rubber gloves and stiff brush. Then he thought a large area rug would be a useful way to hide her body. He had used up all his tarps on the other two. Going back into the house he decided his living room rug would be large enough. Back out in the garage, he laid the rug out flat on the floor. Before opening the side door of his van, he made sure his neighbors wouldn't have a clear view of what he was about to do. He had angled his van in such a way he could remove the body and place her on the rug. She was still unconscious, making it easy to pull a plastic bag over her head and then tie a piece of rope around it. Finally, he rolled her up and placed her back in the van; none of his neighbors would have any clue what he was doing. She wouldn't be able to move her arms and eventually would suffocate. Snug as a bug in a rug.

Everything loaded, he placed a phone call to his buddy in Maryland to let him know he was on his way.

With just a little traffic Eddie arrived at the Hawthorne-Green Funeral Home in Columbia, Maryland three and a half hours later. He was hungry, tired, and just wanted to drop and go, but his buddy Ernie was in the mood to talk and said he needed help loading the body because his assistant was out sick.

"We are really trying to get this chemical cremation accepted as a standard practice here, but we're getting a lot of push back from religious groups" Ernie began as he and Eddie loaded the rug wrapped body of Maybeth Roberts on the gurney.

"We've only been able to use the alkaline hydrolysis container we bought to dispose of people's dogs- that's big business here." Ernie continued as they pushed the body inside the special room where the AH unit was set up.

"If you want a person legally bio-cremated you have to go to Florida, Illinois, Maine or Minnesota. I just don't get why people aren't more open to AH. It's just like natural decomposition only much faster. The end result is a sterile solution and can be disposed of right down the drain. It is totally harmless. There are some bone fragments at the end that we put in the cremulator. Oh, by the way, I still have the bone ash from the last two you brought in. What do you want me to do with that?"

Eddie's mind was numb from the drive and had to shake his head a bit before he answered. "Oh, just throw it out. You told me last time there wasn't any DNA or RNA left so no one would be able to identify the remains, right?"

"Yeah, that's right. Fine, I'll just put it in the trash. Anyway, as I was saying, alkaline hydrolysis was legalized in 2010 but the public doesn't consider it a dignified way of disposing of a loved one even though it's the most kind to the environment. You know it's just fucked up that they think setting their loved ones on fire is OK. I just don't get people, you know. Did you know a standard cremation releases mercury into the air which is harmful? Imagine living next to a funeral home that runs a crematorium and having mercury floating around when you are playing with your kids in the backyard. Plus think of the costs of a traditional burial. Coffins range from five hundred to twenty thousand dollars, then you have the lead or concrete case that surrounds the coffin."

Eddie didn't want to hear anymore; he already had learned more than he wanted to.

"Can we just get this over with Ernie? I'm tired, I need food and I have at least a three-hour drive back home."

"Sure, sure" said Ernie as he opened the round door of the stainless-steel vessel, pulled out the mesh tray and put it on the table. Unlatching the tray at the side, he swung it open and said "Eddie, let's unwrap her and weigh her on this scale."

After noting her weight on the readout, they placed her body in the tray, then latched it shut. The body and tray were slid into the container. Ernie entered the weight into the machine, calculated and measured out the amount of dry potassium hydroxide and sodium hydroxide then added the mixture inside the machine with the body. Closing the door, he said "You have to know the exact weight of the corpse and use the precise amount of chemicals to properly decompose the body."

He then turned a lever and the long stainless-steel tube tilted to about a forty-five degree angle. Pressing a button, water began to enter the tube. "Inside there is a little propeller that pushes the water and chemicals around the body. In about eight hours, she will be history. And, by the way, you can transfer my fee to this account" said Ernie as he pulled a piece of paper from his pocket and handed it to Eddie. "That's fifteen grand, five grand a piece. Are you expecting any more disposals?"

Eddie took the paper and on his way out said, "I hope not, but you never know. It's a pleasure as always to do business with you Ernie. Hope you don't mind if I do a bit of clean-up of my van in your parking lot."

"Better yet, I will open the bay doors to the garage, and you can work inside where no one can see you" offered Ernie. "Our hearses are out at a funeral all day today, so you have plenty of room and privacy."

CHAPTER 17

October 3, 2018

That fall, Miranda and Jack were traveling to Napa, California during the first week in October with two other couples. Jack's brother and wife, Doug and Mary Craig and a couple they had known for years, Ed and Jennifer Rollings. Usually, Jack would go by himself or with his brother, but this year it was going to be a big group event touring several wineries to celebrate Miranda and Jack's twenty-fifth wedding anniversary. Miranda was looking forward to staying in San Francisco for a few days before taking the group's rental van to Napa for the remaining four days.

Because of the hectic rush to get to Newark Airport, the long TSA lines and wait at their Alaska Airlines gate, Miranda had been able to keep her last conversation with Celia off her mind. But now, buckled in her business class seat, all the issues came flooding back. The missing tenant, or possibly two if the old man wandering off counts, and the many complaints from the tenants.

Miranda had been trying to educate herself about mail, online and phone scams. It seemed like the criminals were developing ways to defraud victims faster than law enforcement could shut them down. Why even Jack had received a letter in the mail not too long ago that caused them to be a little concerned. It read:

'Hello Jack, I'm going to cut the chase. I know about the secret you are keeping from your wife. More importantly, I have evidence of what you have been hiding. I won't go into the specifics here in case your wife intercepts this, but you know what I am talking about.

You don't know me personally and nobody hired me to look into you. Nor did I go out looking to burn you. It's just your bad luck that I stumbled across your misadventures while working a job around Warren. I then put in more time than I probably should have looking into your life. Frankly, I am ready to forget all about you and let you get on with your life. And I am going to give you two options that will accomplish that very thing. Those two options are to either ignore this letter, or simply pay me $3,500. Let's examine those two options in more detail.

Option 1 is to ignore this letter. Let me tell you what will happen if you chose this path. I will take this evidence and send it to your wife. And as insurance against you intercepting it before your wife gets it, I will also send copies to her friends and family. So, Jack, even if you decide to come clean with your wife, it won't protect her from the humiliation she will face when her friends and family find out your sordid details from me.

Option 2 is to pay me $3,500. We'll call this my 'confidentiality fee.' Now let me tell you what happens if you choose this path. Your secret remains your secret. You go on with your life as though none of this ever happened. Though you may want to do a better job at keeping your misdeeds secret in the future.

At this point you may be thinking, 'I'll just go to the cops.' Which is why I have taken steps to ensure this letter cannot be traced back to me. So that won't help, and it won't stop the evidence from destroying your life. I'm not looking to break your bank. I just want to be compensated for the time I put into investigating you. $3,500 will close the books on that.

Let's assume you have decided to make all this go away and pay me the confidentiality fee. In keeping with my strategy to not go to jail, we will not meet in person and there will be no physical exchange of cash. You will pay me anonymously using bitcoin. If you want to keep your secret then send $3,500 in BITCOIN to the Receiving Bitcoin Address listed below. Payment MUST be received within 10 days of the post marked date on this letter's envelope. If you are not familiar with bitcoin, attached is 'How-To' guide. You will need the below two pieces of information when referencing this guide.

Tell no one what you will be using the bitcoin for or they may not give it to you. The procedure to obtain bitcoin can take a day or two so don't put it off. Again, payment must be received within 10 days of this letter's post marked date. If I don't receive the bitcoin by the deadline, I will go ahead and release the evidence to everyone. If you go that route, then the least you could do is tell your wife so she can come up with an excuse to prepare her friends and family before they find out. The clock is ticking, Jack."

The second page of the letter had detailed instructions for making the Bitcoin arrangements.

Miranda and Jack did not believe a word that was said in the letter. What disturbed them was the use of Jack's full name and address. As a good citizen, Miranda thought it was her duty to report it to the Warren Police Department but was told by one of the officers there was nothing they could do to trace the letter. He suggested they just ignore it, so they did. What really concerned Miranda was that some dupe with something to hide would actually send the money to this scammer.

Miranda leaned into Jack after their plane took off and whispered in his ear, "Jack, I really hope they find those two people while we are away. Celia is worrying herself sick over this."

"I know you are too, but there is nothing you can do, so sit back, order a drink, take a nap or watch a movie. It's time to have some fun." Just then, the flight attendants began making their way down the aisle with the drink cart.

Miranda took Jack's suggestion and ordered a double, spicy Bloody Mary. Taking a long sip, she put her head back against the seat's pillow and swallowed what seemed like an awful amount of vodka. She immediately began to feel its effects, more so since their flight was just after the butt crack of dawn. Jack didn't like to 'burn daylight' and always booked the earliest flights possible so they would arrive at their destination with time to enjoy at least part of the day.

When she was about halfway through her drink, Jack nudged her while handing her a wrapped box.

"I got you a little present for our anniversary. I knew you would be bored on the flight and probably ruminate all the way to California."

Miranda unwrapped the box to find an iPad and stylish case.

"It's all charged up and ready to use. You can watch something on Netflix or Hulu, email the kids, check out Facebook, read one of your novels- I transferred all your Kindle books. If you find you don't like to read on this, I'll transfer them back. You can also take pictures, but your phone might be easier. I even thought you might want to start a blog or a travelogue. You used to write down all the details of our family vacations; where we stayed, what we did and what we ate. This might be a great opportunity to do that again. I can just imagine you and the kids trying to recreate some of the meals we are going to have on this trip. Plus, it might keep your mind off of Somerville and on Napa."

"Oh Jack! Thank you, this is great! Can you show me how to turn it on?"

"Well, maybe if you kiss it here on that corner..."

Miranda spent the rest of the flight playing with her new toy; watching a movie, emailing the kids and without Jack seeing, jotting down notes of all the facts she knew regarding the disappearances.

Jack had the whole vacation mapped out and scheduled to the minute. He had hotel reservations for each location, restaurants for each meal and as many wine tastings he could schedule in a day without killing them with alcohol poisoning. During the flight, the group was beginning to call him the Napa Nazi. It was looking to be an alcohol fueled getaway, requiring a hollow leg, ability to run on little sleep and the patience of a saint. And as Miranda remembered from previous visits, once they got to Napa and the hills of many of the wineries, there would be no cell service, so hopefully they wouldn't need an ambulance if they ate or drank too much.

Once in San Francisco, they found their hotel in the financial district and checked in. They were famished from the five-and-a-half-hour flight, so they decided to walk the short distance to the Ferry Building Marketplace on the Embarcadero. Hog Island Oyster Company was their first stop on their roadway to gluttony. There was the initial rush of reviewing the menu, getting the wine and dishes ordered and finally, they all exhaled and took in their surroundings.

Looking out the long line of windows facing the waterfront, ferries could be seen coming in from Alcatraz or Sausalito. People were walking about, dodging birds or the homeless, with the Oakland Bay Bridge in the background.

When the food and drinks were on the table and Miranda began sampling everything, she thought to herself, 'I better start that travel and food blog.' She took a few photos of the group, the menu and the marvelous dishes they had ordered and sent off an email to her kids, Kevin and Erica. They were, hopefully, studying away at college or in Kevin's case- in London.

Everything was excellent. They sipped on a local Chardonnay while eating grilled oysters three different ways, beer battered rockfish sliders, grilled cheese made with Cowgirl Creamery Cheese (probably purchased at its store front within the terminal), and grilled squid salad. What a way to start the trip! She made notes about the ingredients in each dish, how it was prepared and served, and especially how each dish tasted. Maybe if this apartment thing did not pan out she could submit articles to magazines like Conde Nast Traveler.

After walking around the shops of the Ferry Building and getting tickets for the next day to take the ferry to Sausalito, they went back to the hotel for a quick nap before dinner.

Of course, Jack had reservations that evening at the Slanted Door, a wonderful Vietnamese restaurant again at the Ferry Building. He knew they would be tired after their flight and late lunch, so he booked the table for six thirty that night which equated to nine thirty Eastern time. It would take a day or two to adjust to the Pacific Time Zone.

The waitress was delivering their extensive order of crispy imperial rolls with gulf shrimp; pork shoulder, vermicelli noodles and roasted peanuts to wrap in Bibb lettuce; spicy grilled pork lettuce wraps with spring onions, mint, and cilantro; cubed filet mignon with watercress, red onion in a lime sauce; stir fried chicken with cashews, walnuts, Chinese dates, raisins and cilantro and don't forget the caramelized shrimp with garlic, yellow onion, chili sauce and jasmine rice when Miranda's phone rang.

Keslie Patch-Bohrod

CHAPTER 18

Celia knew the Craig's were away in California on vacation and hated the idea of calling Miranda to tell her about the most recent events. It had been a busy afternoon showing a couple a number of the vacant rental units and she arrived home later than usual. When her doorbell rang, her first thought was that Greg had forgotten his key. To her surprise Mike O'Ryan was standing there when she opened the door. Inviting him in, he began to ask her if she or Greg had any more openings he could fill. Celia thought this was peculiar because he usually called or emailed. She told him there might be a few opening up but would check with Greg when he got home. Mike thanked her and left.

About fifteen minutes later, Greg arrived home carrying two bags of Thai take-out for their dinner.

"What a great surprise! You know how much I love Origin Thai food. I hope you got me that crispy Peking duck salad I love so much" asked Celia as she put plates and silverware on the table.

"I sure did, I also got Pad Thai, the wild boar and a new shrimp dish I can't pronounce." Greg laid the food containers out on their dining room table and began spooning the food on their plates.

"Greg, I hate to bring this up over such a lovely dinner, but how well do you really know Mike O'Ryan and who is that big, ugly guy that hangs around him?"

Greg put down his fork and thought for a minute. "I guess I really don't know much about him just that we used to go to the same high school. He seems to be doing all right by us; he is really helping to fill our units. As for that big guy, his name is Eddie and he handles some of the tech stuff for him. Why?"

"Oh, Mike stopped by here of all places, about half an hour ago asking if we had any empty units he could fill. It just seemed weird. And on top of that, Detective Morris came by today asking questions about one of the tenants in the Craig's apartment building that has gone missing. That's two missing people from this building. When Mike came by, it was like he knew there was a vacancy."

"That's probably coincidence," Greg conjectured. "Mike is just a go-getter and wants to stay on top of things."

When they were done eating their meal, Celia said, "I'm going to call Miranda out in California. It's about seven o'clock there, so hopefully I won't be interrupting anything. You might want to listen in when I pass along all the details the detective shared with me." Greg said he would, and they both sat next to each other on the couch while Celia made the call.

"Miranda, I am so sorry to bother you again but something else has happened" began Celia.

"What do you mean something else?" asked Miranda after excusing herself from the table and walking outside to better hear Celia.

"The police came by this afternoon looking for information about one of our tenants, Maybeth Roberts. Her boyfriend contacted them when he received a crazy and disturbing email from her. He became more distressed when she wouldn't answer his many phone calls and is convinced something horrible has happened to her. He even had his sister call her and they were best friends, with still no answer. She apparently has been missing a few days, so they searched her apartment, took her computer and impounded her car," explained Celia. "The latest, after accessing her computer, they found her passwords changed, money transferred from her checking and investment accounts, her Social Security benefits re-routed and all her utilities for her apartment shut down. Suspicion falls to the boyfriend; they believe he stole her money and killed her. Reporting it to the police, he hoped it would draw attention away from him. He has been arrested. They need us to stay out of the apartment until they have a chance to go through everything."

"Celia, this is so crazy; two tenants in our apartment building that basically just disappear. Although it appears there is no connection since the police seem to have evidence against the boyfriend."

"Miranda, it does seem that the boyfriend was involved with her disappearance but what really bothers me was that her utilities were all shut down and her accounts transferred. Just like Allister Foley's!"

74

"You are right Celia. That is a coincidence. Could that boyfriend know Allister too?" asked Miranda.

"I don't know, but the police have the information on both cases, so if there is a real connection, they will hopefully find it," replied Celia.

"Please keep me posted, we will be back Monday and can figure out what to do then. Thanks for all you are doing on your end." Miranda hung up the phone and blew out a breath. She went back inside and sat down. She turned to Jack and the group and began to fill them in on what Celia just told her.

After Celia hung up the phone, she turned to Greg and said, "What do you think? Coincidence?"

Greg sat and thought a few minutes, finished his glass of wine and took their plates into the kitchen. As he was loading the dirty dishes into the dishwasher, he finally said to Celia, "I'm beginning to see your point. There is definitely something fishy going on; two people missing from the Craig's apartment building and Mike coming by asking if there were any openings. I think we need to keep our eyes and ears open, and our mouths shut until we know something concrete. Make sure no one can overhear your conversations about this with Miranda, the police or me. If something bad has happened to these people, we have to be careful the same thing doesn't happen to us."

Celia put her dishes in the dishwasher then put her arms around Greg for a hug. She was frightened and she felt relieved he too saw a connection.

After a minute she pulled back from the embrace and said, "Greg, what should we do about Mike?"

"Let's keep an eye on him; just don't let on that you suspect him of anything."

Keslie Patch-Bohrod

CHAPTER 19

Day two in California started with the hotel breakfast buffet then the walk to the terminal for the ferry to Sausalito. It was a beautiful California day, sun shining, no humidity, perfect for the trek to the boat. Miranda couldn't keep her mind off the conversation from the previous night and hearing the concern in Celia's voice and the news of yet another disappearance. Miranda's stress level triggered a hot flash. She felt it deep in her stomach as if someone had lit a match to her internal furnace and the heat quickly spread to the rest of her body. Sweat began to trickle down her face.

Jack noticed and asked, "Miranda, what is it? Are we walking too fast for you? Your face is all wet."

"God, how I hate menopause," admitted Miranda. "The littlest thing sets off a hot flash and it feels like I am on fire. I was just thinking about Celia and that poor woman that went missing and wham on with the flames!"

The only thing Miranda knew to do was to stop, close her eyes and begin to take deep, cleansing breaths, willing her body to cool down. Thankfully, she had a few minutes to do just that while waiting for the ferry. Pulling out her new iPad, she added Celia's new information to her Somerville document and finished her thoughts about last night's dinner. Vietnamese cuisine was really taking off; she especially liked the use of fish sauce, lime, lemongrass, ginger, mint and bird's eye chilis.

Miranda had anticipated Sausalito to be a quaint town, bustling with activity but found it somewhat deserted. Many of the shops were empty or closed with only a few people like themselves walking around. While looking inside one of the stores, the group began to chat with the owner, commiserating about the slow business in the town, noting the number of closed shops. Even though it was a beautiful day, there was little foot traffic. Speculating the time of year as the cause, they changed the subject to lunch recommendations. If seafood and outdoor dining was to their liking, the owner suggested the short walk to Fish at the marina. The couples agreed it sounded like a great idea and headed in the right direction.

After walking about fifteen minutes and deep in thought, Miranda turned to Jack and said, "I need to call the Somerville Police Department and see what is going on. I know that Celia is concerned about those two tenants, but she may not be comfortable enough calling the police and asking some questions. Do we have any idea how much farther this restaurant is?"

Jack yelled ahead to his brother who was following a map on his cell phone, "Hey Doug! How much farther?"

To which his brother replied, "I think that woman was mad that we didn't buy anything in her store. This app says we have two more miles to walk!"

"Well, I guess I have a few minutes to make a call while we walk" said Miranda as she searched for the number in her contacts list of the police officer who had investigated the so-called disappearance of Allister.

When he answered the phone, she said, "Detective Morris, this is Miranda Craig. I don't know if you remember me, but I am the owner of the apartment building where Allister Foley went missing. I also understand from my property manager that another tenant, Maybeth Roberts has also gone missing, and that you have someone in custody. Is there any connection between the two?"

"Yes, of course Mrs. Craig I remember you. Our tech people are still trying to get access to Mr. Foley's accounts, and no one has heard from him since we all met. My men have spoken with the other tenants near his unit, and no one remembers anyone being around his apartment on that day."

"We are still investigating the disappearance of Ms. Roberts. Her friend Rex Martin states emphatically that he had nothing to do with her missing funds and is concerned that something has happened to her as well. He is still in custody but as we investigate him more thoroughly, we are finding reason to believe him. He has an alibi for the approximate time period when she would have gone missing, notably the time after she sent her email. We also found a notebook nearby with all her passwords and accounts that would make it really easy for someone to transfer her accounts."

"Detective, did you find Mr. Foley's laptop or computer? I know he has been sending emails so I assume he must have one or at least a smart phone. Or is there any way we can confirm that he was the one that actually cancelled his accounts? Have you fingerprinted our maintenance people and Celia to make sure it wasn't one of them? I don't have any reason to suspect Celia or our people, but I would assume you would be thorough in checking everyone out."

"I assure you Mrs. Craig, we are doing everything we can. I will keep you posted." And with that, Detective Morris rang off.

The group finally made it to the marina and wound their way around a number of parking lots and buildings until they found the elusive entrance to the restaurant. They each placed their orders at the counter, paid and then found an empty picnic table to await the delivery of their food by the wait staff.

It was a beautiful, sunny day in California. The rustic tables were set up overlooking the marina. The air was fresh, and the sounds of the waterfront were welcoming. Waves lapping against the docks, seagulls 'ha-ha-haing,' boat engines puttering and people talking as they ate.

The food arrived and like the other meals they enjoyed so far it was exceptionally good. They gorged on Pasta con Vongole with homemade egg pasta and garlic, olive oil and pepperoncino; beer battered Alaskan true cod with potato wedges and fish tacos Adobada (which meant marinated) with red chilies, corn tortillas, pickled onions and crema. And of course, Jack had to order two bottles of crisp, cold Chablis to accompany the feast.

They were so stuffed from all the food and with only thirty minutes until the next ferry back to San Francisco, an Uber was the only option to make it back in time. They certainly did not want to stay longer in Sausalito; they had seen as much as they wanted to.

After boarding the return ferry, Miranda found a seat in the sunshine and watched as the vessel pulled away from the dock. Jack and the rest of the group were standing near the bow of the boat taking in the bay and chatting about the dinner reservations for that night. Oh boy, thought a full and sleepy Miranda. More food and wine!

Being away from prying eyes, Miranda seized the opportunity to update her notes. If it wasn't the boyfriend, who could it be?

That night they entered a small, touristy restaurant, in the Fisherman's Wharf district. The hostess led the group to the main dining room on the other side of the bar area. Large mirrors flanked one wall, artificially inflating the actual size of the room. The tables were close together, which became problematic when a server ignited an order of bananas foster right behind Miranda. With her insurance background and long ponytail near the flames, the liability issues overshadowed any positive views of the restaurant in her mind.

She just could not get into the right frame of mind to enjoy herself. Thoughts of her catching on fire, missing tenants, and Celia having to hold down the fort all by herself really put a damper on Miranda's vacation. She kept telling herself there was nothing she or Celia could do at this point, neither disappearance was their fault and the police promised they were doing all they could to locate these people.

CHAPTER 20

Day three started early driving out of San Francisco to start one of many winery tours. Gloria Ferrer Caves and Vineyards was in Sonoma and was known for its Spanish style sparkling wines and sustainability practices. Like most of the Sonoma and Napa wineries, the view as well as the wine was worth the price of the Classic Carneros tasting of four sparkling wines. And no tasting was complete without the cheese and wafer plate.

The River Terrace Inn, located in downtown Napa, overlooked the Napa River. Jack selected this hotel based on its walking distance to the Oxbow Market where they would select their lunch items to accompany their next tasting in the hills of St. Helena.

Amizetta Estate Winery sat at the base of Howell Mountain, which did not make sense to Miranda because of the long, upward, winding drive to the vineyard. The breathtaking views of Lake Hennessey, Pritchard Hill and San Pablo Bay from the outdoor tasting venue only added to the 'complexity' of their wines. This was the first time the others had the opportunity to experience the Craig's favorite winery, and it wouldn't be the last of this trip. For their last night in Napa, they had been invited to a special Harvest Party which promised to be spectacular.

Dinner that night was at Coles Chop House in Napa City. Miranda thought after this week of major overindulgence, she would have to starve herself for a month. Oh, and her poor liver, what could she do about that? Thank goodness Jack hired a driver for their winery visits. Buzz was a great guy and was well acquainted with all the wineries, getting them to and from safely.

Day four included tastings at the David Arthur, Ballentine and Reverie Wineries and dinner at Celadon back in Napa City. Each winery had its own style when presenting their various white and red wines. The vintner liked to point out the wine's appearance in the glass, how it smelled in the glass, the taste impressions, where the taste hit within the mouth and how the wine finished after the sip was complete. David Arthur Winery had a long, wooden table under a giant tree providing shade, reminiscent of being in Tuscany.

Ballentine was much more simplistic, so your mind and pallet were focused on the wine only. Reverie was fun and brought back memories of hiding out in the woods, drinking with college friends in rustic chairs, the family dog and lovely views.

To end the evening, dinner was at Caledon's courtyard in downtown Napa. After such a long day, Miranda could barely keep her eyes open, much less remember what she ate. There would be a gap in her travelogue tonight. All she wanted to do was to go to bed.

Would this Bacchanalia ever end?

In the morning, as they were leaving the hotel, Miranda thought back to the summer. It was still hard to believe she had been in the middle of a cyberwar plot in their little New Jersey shore town. Was she involved in another situation now? What kept bothering her was why did seemingly contented people all of a sudden become 'discontented' and vanish? One, maybe. Two, highly unlikely.

"Jack," said Miranda as their driver was pulling the van into the parking lot of the day's first tasting. "I am worried about Celia and what is going on back home."

After thinking for a minute Jack said, "Maybe you should call John Franklin and run it by him, see what he thinks."

Their last full day and night started with a tour and tasting at Chateau Montelena Winery, made famous by the Judgment of Paris and the movie *Bottle Shock*. This was a beautiful winery and very commercial, probably influenced by the notoriety of the movie and how they had helped put Napa and California on the map for wine connoisseurs.

The grounds surrounding the Chateau were lush and green. At the entrance was a large tasting bar and selection of various items for purchase. When it came time for their tasting to begin, they were led into a large kitchen with a center island much like Miranda's in her shore house, seating at least ten people. They were only six, so two more couples would be joining them. They tasted a 2017 Riesling, 2010 Chardonnay, 2012 Zinfandel, 2009 Cabernet Sauvignon and a 2006 Cabernet Sauvignon. The only time they ever used the sip and spit urn next to them during their trip was when a wine was bad. Maybe that was why the use of a driver was essential for them. They rarely found a wine they didn't like, and they finished every last drop.

The tour and tasting ended about twelve-thirty and they were able to make their one o'clock lunch reservation at Solbar, part of the Solage Auberge Resorts in Calistoga. Needless to say, when they reached their lunch destination, they were a bit tipsy.

Jack had arranged for a representative from Fisher Winery to prepare a wine flight while they had lunch at the restaurant. The best dishes were the farm fresh heirloom tomatoes with burrata cheese, and shrimp lettuce wraps with spicy avocado, pickled carrots and nampala dipping sauce.

The highlight of the evening and the perfect ending to their vacation was the Harvest Party at Amizetta Winery. Loads of people, music, barbeque and of course wine! Miranda knew Amizetta wines were Jack's favorite and that he bought cases, but she didn't realize how much of a benefit that would turn out to be. The Harvest Party was a yearly event for the winery and apparently wine club members could secure one of the limited number of invitations by calling on a certain day.

Miranda, with a glass of Chardonnay in hand, found a seat with a spectacular view of the valley. The band was finalizing its setup and microphone checks when another woman sat down nearby.

"Don't you just love this place? I had to get up at four o'clock in the morning and start calling in order to buy tickets for this party. How long did it take you?

"Tickets?" questioned Miranda.

"Yes, you have to be a wine club member and buy a ticket, but it's limited. The line was busy for hours then I finally got through and was able to secure two tickets for my husband and me. How long have you been a club member?"

Miranda giggled and said, "Oh, we aren't wine club members. My husband just loves the wine, especially the Complexity."

"Well then how are you here?" the woman growing more indignant.

"Maybe it's the thirty cases of wine my husband orders over the year."

When the woman heard the amount of wine Jack usually ordered, she spit out a bit of wine she just sipped and said, "THIRTY CASES!?"

"Like I said," Miranda repeated, "he really loves the wine." At that point, the rest of Miranda's group joined them, made introductions and suggested they get in line for the barbeque buffet.

Tables had been set up inside the winery tasting room and outside the vat room. As the guests lined up to get their food, Miranda shared the conversation she had had with the woman they just met. The group laughed and patted Jack on the back thanking him for the invitation because of his overindulgence in the wine.

As the night wore on, more wine was consumed, funny stories shared and the strings of twinkling lights turned the evening into a fairytale event. The winery owner, Spencer, joined the band singing and playing guitar; rumored that growing up in Texas, he used to play guitar with a famous 60s and 70s rock and roll band.

When their car service arrived to take them back to their hotel, the group collected their parting gifts of a bottle of wine and chocolates and said their goodbyes to their hosts. It had been a spectacular finish to their Napa and San Francisco visit.

On the plane back home that next day, Miranda was determined to call John Franklin. He had been so helpful over the summer; she was sure he would have suggestions. She made notes on her tablet of the key points regarding the disappearances so she would not forget to mention them.

CHAPTER 21

Karen Sinclair wanted to get out of her current apartment as soon as possible. She had lived there for several years but now that she retired from the Bridgewater, New Jersey school system, she was anxious to move into an apartment community with older residents and no children.

Her rent had been increasing steadily over the years and she felt she could find an apartment of better value. With all the new apartment complexes going up, she was certain to find one within her price range and with a wide range of amenities.

Having taught Algebra and Calculus at the high school level for over twenty-five years, and earning her master's degree, she had been at the top of the pay scale. She had to thank their teachers' union for negotiating a great pension plan for its members. During the summer months she had worked for several different companies, like Target and Walmart, because she liked to keep busy but also to make extra money.

Her pension benefits began shortly after the school year ended in June, giving her a few months to begin saving for a move. She had recently gone into the Social Security office to register and to begin the meager benefits she had accumulated through her various part time jobs. She noticed an advertisement on the bulletin board for a beautiful, one bedroom apartment near downtown Somerville which listed many pluses for senior citizens. Her Social Security benefits and part of her pension would cover the monthly rent of this unit. As soon as she got home, she

pulled out her cell phone and dialed the number from the poster.

"O'Ryan Realty Placement Services, how may I help you?" answered Mike O'Ryan.

"Hi, my name is Karen Sinclair and I saw your advertisement at the Social Security office for an apartment in Somerville. Is it still available?"

"That is one our most popular apartments, I know we have had at least six other inquiries and visits within the last two days. I will have to check with the owner of the building to see if it has been rented yet. If you are really interested you may want to put down a deposit to make sure you get it, even before you see it; these one bedrooms go so fast. But first, I would appreciate a little information about yourself so I can call you back, and if it is already rented, I can also tell you about other rentals we have available."

Karen obliged, giving him her name and phone number.

As part of his normal speech to prospective tenants, Mike added, "Are you moving from another apartment or home, and will you have a roommate or any pets?" Mike wanted to maximize his options and minimize any problems, if at all possible. Single, unencumbered tenants were best, and by no means did he want a dog that would attack them when they entered the apartment on their rounds.

"I am moving from an apartment; the rent was getting quite high. I just retired from teaching and the price advertised for this property is well within my budget. I will not have a roommate and don't plan on a pet. In case I change my mind, is this apartment building pet friendly?" asked Karen.

"Yes, small dogs under forty pounds and cats are allowed with a pet security deposit of two hundred and fifty dollars and an additional twenty-five a month added to the rental payments. This helps cover the wear and tear those animals cause over the life of the lease."

"That sounds reasonable," responded Karen.

"Well, Mrs. Sinclair, oh I am sorry, are you a Miss or a Mrs.? I want to make sure to address you properly," said Mike conciliatorily.

Giggling, Karen said, "Oh I am just a Miss, never got around to getting married. I guess that makes me an old maid. I was just more interested in teaching than meeting the right man and settling down."

"Of course, Miss Sinclair, I will get in touch with the owner and call you back by the end of the day. Will that work for you?" Mike wanted time to research this new prospect. So far, so good. Pension, social security, no pets, no man and in need of a new apartment. He had not planned on the boyfriend with the last tenant they took care of, but luck would have it, the police suspected him.

"I just have a few more questions if you will. When are you planning to move in and what is the name of your current apartment? I will need to run a credit check on you as part of our lease requirements."

"I would like to move in by November first, if possible, that is when my current lease expires. I know I am cutting it a bit close, my landlord at Waterside Garden Apartments said they would let me stay on another month if needed. I am sure you will find that I am a good credit risk and I will supply you all the information you need once we secure the apartment."

"Great," replied Mike. "I will be in touch later today. Thanks for calling." Mike hung up the phone and called Eddie into his office to give him the task of vetting Karen Sinclair.

Once Eddie left, Mike went back to his earlier activities. He had been so busy finding rentals for Greg Baker and scheming ways to make money off them. Most were direct deposits for their monthly rental, but for one reason or another, he had to proceed with caution dealing with most of those renters. Only Celia's tenants so far had been easy, quick marks.

Mike had been working with Greg since the spring. Seven of Greg's tenants had been taken care of, quickly finding replacements after they died of natural causes or vacated their property. Greg was none the wiser and had not really paid attention or called when he had the turnover. Mike guessed it was because he owned so many units and this was a turnover he would expect. Thankfully, Greg had Celia working primarily on the Craig building so she was not physically around so much with his other properties. Mike made a mental note to monitor her a bit more closely just to make sure she too was clueless.

The natural deaths in Greg's buildings came too fast for Mike to take full advantage of the situation. He had only been able to skim a bit from the direct deposits and from some of the accounts. He had to be careful not to alert the authorities by wiping out full accounts mere minutes after the tenant died.

Back to the task at hand, he picked up the phone and punched in the number. "Hey Celia, it's Mike O'Ryan. How are you? Listen, I have someone interested in your building; do you still have that one bedroom on the third floor available?"

"I sure do, if you want to send someone around to see it, set it up for me for tomorrow at ten o'clock in the morning, OK?" asked Celia

"Will do, thanks!"

Celia hung up the phone and began to think about what Mike just said. 'How could he know I had a one bedroom available on the third floor? We just got that emptied and cleaned up after Maybeth left.' She began to worry more and more about Mike O'Ryan.

Miranda got up early on the morning after their return from California. She showered, dressed, ate a quick breakfast and headed straight to the apartment building to see Celia.

Greeting Celia as she walked in the door, she said, "Hi Celia. I am finally back and here to help. Have you learned anything new since my phone call to Detective Morris?"

"It's great to have you back Miranda! How was the trip? Are you still drunk?" joked Celia.

"It was wonderful. I am sure if I were breathalyzed right now, I would still be over the legal limit. But seriously, I am really worried about you and what is going on," said Miranda.

"I'm beginning to obsess over these disappearances, but I have to keep telling myself that I'm probably reading too much into things," admitted Celia. "Bad things happen to people every day. People change their minds all the time. Things happen that derail long term plans. But what has really started to concern me is that Mike O'Ryan seems to know when there are openings even before I tell him."

"Celia, maybe he sees people moving out or other tenants tell him. Could Greg be telling him what's going on?" asked Miranda.

"I don't think so" replied Celia. "Greg's been so busy he's had me contact Mike about his vacancies."

"Anything new on Allister?" asked Miranda.

"I haven't received any more emails from Mr. Foley, and since I haven't heard from Mr. Newman, I am assuming he hasn't either. At this point, I am just moving on. We recently got a new tenant, a wonderful woman named Karen Sinclair. I hope you get a chance to meet her. I think you will really like her."

"Just keep me posted on any new developments. In the meantime, I will be around for a while to help out."

"Sounds good to me," replied Celia. "While you are here, would you mind manning the phones while I go check on some work that the maintenance guys are doing? The blinds needed to be replaced in one of the units and I want to make sure that it gets done today."

"I would be happy to, and Celia, I'm glad things aren't as bad as I have been imagining them to be."

Keslie Patch-Bohrod

CHAPTER 22

Karen fell in love with the cozy apartment and found Celia extremely helpful and friendly. She was anxious to move in as soon as possible, filling out the paperwork right after viewing the unit. The amount of personal and financial data required made her pause, but Celia said they needed that information to run the credit check to make sure she could make the monthly payments once she signed the lease contract. Celia promised the information was secure, that only she and the Craigs, the owners of record, had access to it. She also explained that her Social Security number was required and that if she wanted the convenience of the direct deposit, her bank routing and account numbers would be needed.

Karen really wanted the apartment, so she acquiesced, providing all her financial data. She was glad Celia was handling the paperwork instead of Mike O'Ryan. There was something about his manner and voice she did not trust.

She would be able to move in on her targeted date of November first and her first Social Security check would be deposited directly into her rental account and the remaining funds withdrawn from her personal checking account. She would still owe for some of her utilities and trash removal, but that was minor, considering.

She took immense pride decorating her new place, picking out just the right furniture for the space. Plants, rugs, and knickknacks followed. She began to meet people in the area as well as her building and was pleased as her social activities picked up. This new move was working out better than she had planned. So much had been accomplished in only two weeks, she couldn't believe it!

On her way to pick up her mail at the postal boxes inside the front entrance, she ran into Celia, who was on her cell phone. She overheard part of her conversation.

"Oh honey, don't worry about your friend. I know sometimes girls can be fickle when they get really involved with a new guy, but I am sure we can manage the vacation. I will get the time off and drive down there." There was a pause in the conversation then Celia said, "You know I really hate to fly and besides, there are a few places on the way down I have always wanted to visit so this will give me the chance. Again, don't worry, we will have a ball. Bye Sweetie, I will talk with you later tonight after I get the go ahead from Greg and the Craigs."

Celia hung up the phone, looked at Karen and let out a long breath. "Do you have kids?" she asked.

"Well, over the years I did have several hundred, but thankfully they went home every day to someone else!" Karen laughed.

"Oh, that's right, you were a teacher. Well, my daughter and her roommate were planning a road trip to Key West over their Thanksgiving school break; they both attend University of South Florida in Tampa. The roommate, Beth, met this guy, has fallen head over heels and is bailing on the vacation to spend time with him. Kim, that's my daughter, had already booked the hotel with her credit card and Beth is refusing to pay her share of the cost because she is not going. Kim is distraught, because the hotel is expensive, and they won't give her a refund. The girls were treating themselves for studying so hard and now she has this huge credit card bill. So, I guess I am taking a road trip to Tampa, and then to Key West!" explained Celia.

"What a wonderful mother you are! It sounds like loads of fun. I went years ago with a number of teacher friends, and we really enjoyed it. The weather should be fairly good this time of year too. Hurricane season just ended which is a big plus. How long will you be gone?" asked Karen.

"That's the thing, a normal person would fly to Tampa, and then it would be only a week. But I will not fly; I absolutely refuse to get on a plane. I know I am unreasonable and it is safer than driving, but after 9/11 I just can't face the other passengers without thinking someone is plotting to try to take the plane down. So, I guess I will be gone at least two weeks if I can get the time off."

"I am sure you will have a wonderful time with your daughter. These kinds of trips are what make lifelong memories. I guess I won't see you until well into December?"

"Probably, but everything will be OK here. The maintenance people are wonderful, and you have a direct line should you need anything repaired or have a problem. I will leave my cell phone number on the resident portion of the website, and you can sign on and get it. Please feel free to call me if you have a problem that has not been resolved and I will find someone to take care of it. I guess I better get a hold of my bosses and make sure I can get this time off!" Celia grabbed her own mail from the box. Just before entering her apartment, she turned around and asked," Karen, would you mind telling me when and where you found out about your apartment?"

"Um," Karen paused and thought, "well, if I remember correctly, it was when I applied for my Social Security benefits. I saw a flyer on the bulletin board outside the office detailing the building, amenities and the available unit. I remember seeing that it was a third-floor unit and thinking that would be ideal because I might have a bit of a view outside my window. And, for the timing, it was available just a few weeks before November first. I was really lucky to be able to move in so quickly."

Celia thanked her and went into her apartment. She to thought to herself, 'How did Mike know that particular apartment was available? I hadn't told him we got the go ahead to rent it from the police. Could one of the maintenance men have shared with him that the unit was being cleaned and prepped? Something just doesn't feel right.'

CHAPTER 23

Celia was relieved when Greg and Miranda told her she could have the time off. This was a slow rental period being so close to the holidays; people usually did not want to try to move during this time of year. Maintenance would be the busiest, so she would need to have a talk with them and maybe bribe them to be even more helpful over the Thanksgiving holiday in her absence.

During her conversation with Miranda, she discussed her plan for the maintenance men and Miranda promised to help when she could. Miranda reminded Celia that she too would be away at the end of November. Her cousin's son was getting married in South Carolina and she was flying down for the wedding. She would be available by phone if Celia needed to contact her. If there was an emergency when they both were away, Miranda could rely on Jack to come in and take care of things.

Celia called Kim back and made plans for her arrival in Tampa and set their departure date for the road trip to Key West.

CHAPTER 24

Mike had been staked out in the Starbucks across the street from the Somerville apartment where Karen Sinclair lived. He had an unobstructed view of the parking lot as well as the entrance where most tenants entered.

Getting anxious to go after her money, Mike took it upon himself to track her comings and goings to see if there was a pattern. She tended to go out daily after breakfast, usually around nine in the morning and returning about noon for lunch. Only on Thursday afternoons did she leave again for a standing manicure appointment which lasted only one hour.

As he was noting her daily movements over a two-week period, he would work on his computer in Starbucks ordering coffee and sometimes lunch. The baristas didn't bother him as there were a number of other patrons who also spent large amounts of time making the store a makeshift office. Some even held business meetings at the larger tables.

Mike thought he had enough data and felt secure enough to tell Eddie to go into her apartment that morning shortly after she left in her car. The plan was to look for passwords hidden around her computer or desk. Then install spyware so they could remotely access her computer. When the time was right, they would wipe out all of her accounts. Believing he had some time to himself, he got up from his little table by the window, went to the bathroom then ordered another grande latte. He was sitting down taking a sip of his extremely hot coffee when he spotted Karen Sinclair's car back in the lot.

He threw down the coffee cup, spilling it all over the floor and ran out the door toward the apartment building. There was so much traffic he had to pause before crossing the street, which gave him just enough time to pull out his cell phone from his pocket and call Eddie to warn him.

"Too late!" yelled Eddie as he answered his phone, then he abruptly hung up.

Mike darted out in front of the oncoming traffic which was met with screeching brakes and honking horns. He knew he had to get to her apartment as quickly as possible, knowing the situation could turn ugly very quickly. Again.

"Shit, shit, shit" Mike swore under his breath as he moved from floor to floor on the slow elevator. When he stepped out, he looked both ways to make sure no other tenants were around that could identify him when he entered the woman's apartment.

Opening Karen Sinclair's door slowly, not knowing what to expect, but dreading what he would find, he saw Eddie standing over the woman's body.

"Hey, Mikey, I thought you were on top of things! I was doing just what you told me to do. I was installing that spyware so we could see all her accounts, passwords and emails. Then we would be able to remove her money. I was even going to hide little telltale signs that would point the authorities toward your old business partner Harry, God rest his soul," Eddie said with a little smirk. "We'd be rich, she would be alive, and Harry would take the blame. The police would just assume he disappeared with the loot. If they got wise to Harry's past connection to you, you could just say he was mad how your association had ended, and he was trying to frame you."

"Anyway, I was sitting at her computer, and she walked in and started screaming her head off. You were supposed to be keeping an eye open and watching for her. I would have had time to leave if you called me the minute she drove into the parking lot. Now we have another body to get rid of."

"What did you do when she came in screaming?" asked Mike.

"I ran over to her and put one hand on her mouth to quiet her and the other on the back of her head. She was squirming and thrashing about so much I must have broken her neck. At least there is no blood" explained Eddie as he began shutting down the computer and wiping all the surfaces he had touched.

"We are going to have to wait until the middle of the night when everyone is asleep to move her body to your van. We should get out of here now and meet back at my office to figure out how to move her body," said Mike.

"Wait, I think I have an idea, Mikey. You know she has been doing a lot of shopping for furniture and stuff. How about I go to a furniture store and see if they have a big box I can have? Then later this afternoon, I will dress like a delivery guy, put the box on a hand truck and wheel it to her apartment. I'll pretend like I am talking to her about where to place it in case someone is around and might hear. Then I'll put her in the empty box and wheel her out in broad daylight. Most furniture companies take away the old furniture so that will explain why I had to remove the box with the hand truck."

"That's a great idea," said Mike. "Do you think your guy can manage another body?"

"I will call him while I'm out getting a box" replied Eddie as he closed Karen's door and wiped the knob clean of his prints. He would wipe the rest of the apartment when he returned later.

CHAPTER 25

A week before Celia was scheduled to leave for the south; she thought it was odd that she hadn't seen Karen Sinclair around the building. It seemed like she always ran into her sometime during the day because Karen was usually going somewhere to do fun things. A sense of dread came upon Celia, Karen was in her sixties and older people did have balance issues. Worried she might have fallen in her apartment and couldn't get to a phone, Celia went to her unit and knocked on her door. She called out to her, then listened at the door. With no answer, she slid a note into her mailbox, phoned and left a message for her to call her as soon as she could.

Three days went by, and Celia still hadn't heard from Karen. Really worried at this point, she grabbed the master key from the office and entered the apartment to see if anything was wrong. She would take her chances if Karen were in there and upset with Celia entering her unit.

Celia looked around the apartment, saw there were dirty dishes in the sink, wet clothes in the washer and the bed was not made. Usually, this wouldn't bother Celia, but the food was really dried on the dishes in the sink and the clothes in the washer were beginning to smell musty. She thought Karen was much more conscientious about keeping things clean in her apartment. No one wanted to attract cockroaches and this was a sure way to entice them into your humble abode. Maintenance came in monthly and sprayed as a precautionary measure, but they still had the occasional complaint. She looked around to see if she could find Karen's purse, but it was not there.

Celia went back to her office in her apartment and checked her records for Karen's car and the license plate number. She walked out to the parking lot and was surprised to see the car in the lot.

CHAPTER 26

Not being a statistics wiz but knowing when something happened to three people in a row, Celia understood it was statistically significant. She did not believe in coincidences. It would be one thing if these events happened at different apartment buildings around the city, but at one location? It was too odd. The disappearances all occurred after she started using O'Ryan Realty Placement Services, began direct deposit for rental payments and the tenants had only recently taken possession. Could there be a connection?

She began to wonder about the tenants at Greg's other apartments since, he too used O'Ryan Realty Placement Services. It would only take a few minutes out of her day to run a quick program to determine how many tenants had been referred by the service, which apartment building they were living in, their move in date and if any of them had moved out.

Grabbing her purse and car keys, she ran out to her car and drove to Greg's central office. Thankfully, he wasn't there. She sat down in his chair and turned on his computer.

Greg's system was the same as the one she was using at the Craig's building, making it easy for her to pull up various reports. After tallying and analyzing all the data, Celia found that all of Greg's ten remaining apartment buildings had been using the service. Each building averaged between four and five tenants placed with direct deposit. All the tenants were in one-bedroom apartments and had no roommates or pets. This seemed pretty normal to Celia; most of the people she rented to lease a one bedroom without pets.

She decided to investigate the demographics of the group and was shocked that every single one of them was over sixty-two years old. She checked her listing of the Somerville apartment and found this to also be true. That was a bit strange. Why were so many elderlies targeting these apartments? The past tenants had historically been in the twenty-five to forty age group.

Including this particular building, there were forty-eight residents in the over sixty-two age group, four of which, to her knowledge had died or disappeared.

Could Mike be marketing to an unstable population, around a mental health facility? With the new tenants being of retirement age, maybe he put up multiple flyers near the Social Security office. Karen had said that's where she learned of the apartment. In her mind, Celia thought this age group would be very dependable compared to some of the millennials she had rented to in the past.

She couldn't understand how these outgoing, friendly and positive people, had all of a sudden become so unhappy with their surroundings and apartment, that they would just leave without a trace. What kind of issue would warrant that type of reaction? She hadn't received any complaints from anyone, except regarding those annoying phone calls some of the tenants had been receiving.

Thinking Karen had become ill or injured, she called the local hospital but was unable to get any information because of HIPPA regulations.

More research was needed. Just as Celia began to pull up one of Greg's buildings on the system to conduct an in-depth search of the tenants and their departure dates, Greg walked into the office.

"Celia, can you do me a huge favor? There is a major problem with the swimming pool over at the apartment building near Raritan Valley Community College. Would you be able to run over and meet the pool maintenance company? See what the problem is, have them fix it and cut them a check so they can get the work done as soon as possible? One of my best tenants is planning a pool party for their teenage daughter this weekend and I need to make sure the pool is fixed before then."

"Isn't this a bit late in the season for a pool party?" asked Celia.

"Yes, I guess it is a bit late, but the weather has been unseasonably warm, so I delayed closing the pool and the temperature this weekend is expected to be in the upper seventies. I imagine they want take advantage of that," replied Greg.

Celia grabbed her purse and rose from the desk chair. "Makes sense, I guess. I can run over there right now and take care of it. What time will you be home for dinner tonight?"

Greg thought for a minute then said, "I think I can be home by seven o'clock, but I will call you if something comes up. Thanks for the help. I have a meeting in thirty minutes and really appreciate you jumping in and taking care of this problem."

Celia left the office and decided to stop in the bathroom before she left. As she passed by his office on her way to the parking lot, she noticed Greg staring down at the computer screen. He was on the phone saying something to the person on the other end. It sounded like, "I don't know what it means, but she was looking at the tenant listing page that included date of birth, rental date, referral source and lease termination date."

Before he could turn around and see her standing there, she hustled out of the office, mentally kicking herself for not closing out the program when he came in. It shouldn't be a problem she chided herself; she was given access to all that information. Regardless, she would have to produce a reasonable explanation of what she was looking for. Greg couldn't have an issue with what she was doing, could he? Unless he was up to something.

CHAPTER 27

That night when Celia returned home, Greg was waiting for her at her apartment. Handing her a glass of wine he asked, "What were you researching on the computer today before I asked you to take care of the Raritan pool issue?"

"Hello to you too! First, the pool is fixed; something got clogged in the filter and Max was able to clean it out. He checked the chemicals, and it is good to go for the weekend pool party. As for what I was researching, I just wanted to see how well O'Ryan Placement Services was doing in filling up the apartments. They have been such a great service for the Craig building I was curious to see if and how they were working out for your units." Celia had been thinking all day how she was going to respond to Greg if he had any questions about what she was doing. She didn't know if he was engaged in anything shady and had to be careful about what she told him.

"I thought I would put together a little report for you if you wanted it, or does Mike do that for you?"

Greg replied, "I called him today after I saw the information on the computer. I thought you might have a problem with him. I couldn't ask you because you had left for Raritan and I thought it was easier to just ask him if there was a problem, that way I could manage it. He assured me there were no problems and he was pleased with how well things were going. He said he would send me a report with my placement rates and costs tomorrow, so you don't need to worry about that. But thanks for thinking of it. I have been so busy with this new potential property I haven't been paying attention to much of anything, especially you. And you are going away for two weeks soon. I am sorry. When you get back, we will plan something special. Hopefully, by then, things will quiet down, and we can spend some time together around Christmas. How does that sound?" asked Greg.

"Greg, that would be wonderful, "responded Celia. She got the feeling Greg had forgotten their conversation about Mike or he had been playing along with her concerns. She would keep her thoughts to herself and only share with Miranda if things got worse.

CHAPTER 28

The day before she planned to leave for her trip, Celia overheard Greg talking to Mike. She couldn't quite make out what was being said. They were discussing a new tenant in one of his other buildings and setting up the accounts. Greg said to Mike that he was concerned things may fall through the cracks with Celia being gone for two weeks in Tampa and Key West and hoped Mike could pick up the slack for him.

Celia was still having her suspicions about Mike O'Ryan. Crazy things were happening since they contracted for his services-missing and possibly dead tenants and weird phone calls. Was he responsible for this stuff? He seemed so professional around her and she hadn't received any negative feedback from any of the tenants, specifically about him. So, what was really going on around here?

There was nothing Celia could do about the conversation she overheard in Greg's office other than call Miranda and tell her. She had to get home, get packed and get on the road. Putting herself on a tight schedule to make the drive to Tampa, she would make two stops before arriving at her daughter's apartment. She also went online to MapQuest and planned out her route, wanting to make sure to have printed directions to each of her destinations in case she lost her phone, or the GPS did not work in her car. Panic would strike if she didn't know where to go. Hopefully, the MapQuest directions would be the same as the GPS in her car.

The plan was to first drive to Baltimore and spend the night. One of the items on her bucket list was to see the Inner Harbor and Fells Point. Booking a hotel room right by the Inner Harbor she would be able to walk around, do some shopping and find a wonderful place to have dinner.

After packing and checking that all appliances and ceiling fans were turned off, Celia was able to depart by three o'clock. With Baltimore being a three-hour drive from her apartment, she would arrive at her hotel around six o'clock. She could check in and walk somewhere nice for dinner.

Merging onto the New Jersey Turnpike, Celia decided to call Miranda. The traffic was light enough that she could pay attention to the road and tell Miranda the latest. After exchanging greetings, Celia got down to the purpose of her call.

"Miranda," she began, "I'm afraid something has happened to another tenant. It's been a few days since I last saw Karen Sinclair. Remember how I said I wanted you to meet her?"

"Yes, of course I remember," said Miranda. "What's happened?"

"I'm not sure yet," continued Celia, "but she's not in her apartment. There are dirty dishes in her sink, musty wet clothes in her washer and her car is in our parking lot. When I last spoke to her, I was telling her I was going to the Keys with Kim. We had an enjoyable conversation, and she had no complaints."

"Well, maybe she was called away unexpectantly or someone picked her up for a weekend getaway. Maybe a relative is sick or maybe she got sick?" offered Miranda.

"I thought of that. I even called the hospital but as you know they can't tell you anything. I'm really worried and the fact that I'm going to be away for a while is really stressing me out. I need to find her and make sure she is all right. On top of that, I have been hearing more and more complaints about crazy spam phone calls. You know we have a large number of elderly residents, and they are particularly vulnerable to this kind of fraud."

"Did Karen, Allister or Maybeth ever mention getting strange calls?"

Celia thought a moment and said, "Not that I remember, but they could have."

"Celia, please go on your trip and let me handle this for now. First, I will call the police and report her missing, since she has not been seen in over three days. Second, I will call my friend John Franklin and see if he can refer someone to independently look into these tenants and the phone calls. Not sure what can be done, but another set of eyes might help."

"Thanks, Miranda. I will stay in touch."

Celia made good time on the New Jersey Turnpike and 95 South but as she approached Baltimore and rush hour, she was crawling. Checking into the Courtyard by Marriott hotel at six that night, she was famished. She dropped off her suitcase in her room and made her way down Aliceanna Street to South Broadway. The concierge had given her directions that seemed quite easy.

Thankfully, it was still light outside with the help of the streetlamps, and people were moving along the sidewalks at a good pace. She fell in line with a group that seemed to be headed in the right direction. Fells Point was a popular spot, so she just assumed that was their ultimate destination.

Just before she got to Thames Street, she spotted a cute shop on the left, EC Pops. It was loaded with all sorts of colorful things, but what caught her eye was the number of novelty socks. She purchased a pair with palm trees and another with what looked like rum runner cocktail glasses on them. Kim would love these, she thought.

When she was leaving the store, she saw two men walking quickly down the street, looking carefully at all the tourists. Thinking they must be looking for a friend, she continued to Thames Street, taking a left. She had heard about the Thames Oyster House but when she found it, there was a line outside waiting to get in. Bypassing those waiting in line, Celia asked the hostess how long the wait would be. When the reply was forty-five minutes, she knew she didn't want to wait in a line that long, so she thanked the hostess for the information, turned around and decided to try some of the other drink and snack establishments she had passed along the way.

When she spotted Kooper's Tavern with the image of a golden retriever or yellow lab above the door and on the round sign hanging above it, she decided to give it a try. Celia loved dogs. Inside, all the stools and tables were filled. Looking dismayed, she started to turn around and leave when the bar maid behind the counter yelled to her, "There's plenty of room at the upstairs bar if you are interested."

Celia smiled, turned around and said, "Yes, thanks!" She found the stairs, the upper-level bar and a small table for two right by a window. Perfect. Sitting down, she grabbed a menu that was stuffed between the salt and pepper shakers and the napkin holder. When the bartender asked what she wanted she ordered the Kooper's Crab Dip and whatever he recommended on draft.

The smell of the crab and cheese hit her before the bartender set the plate with the dip and crostini down in front of her. He returned a few minutes later with her draft beer.

Nothing could beat this, she thought; eating crab that was probably caught locally. She dipped a piece of the crusty bread into the gooey mixture and put it in her mouth. As she chewed, she looked out the window at the hundreds of people walking around Thames Street. Not only was she surprised with the number of people outside in November but the number of people with dogs. There weren't just one or two people out walking their dogs like you might expect. There were ten or twenty. As she was trying to count the actual number, she espied another interesting thing. The two men she had spotted earlier were right in front of Kooper's looking around like they had lost something, or someone.

A sudden chill set in. It struck her as odd that she had seen them before and now they were hovering about right below her. She continued eating her snack and drinking her beer, all the while keeping an eye on them. Thinking she must be paranoid, she tried to focus on thoughts of her daughter and how much fun they were going to have on their road trip.

Twenty minutes passed and the men were still standing near the front entrance to the tavern. Even though she didn't think they were looking for her, Celia decided she would find an exit at the back of the bar and wander around a bit more before finding a place to have her dinner.

After 9/11, she not only refused to fly but she was extra aware of her surroundings. She was careful how she held her purse so no one could reach inside for her wallet or snatch it off her shoulder; she also paid attention to people. What they looked like, how they walked, what they carried. These two men were behaving oddly, and Celia wanted to make sure, whatever they were up to, she was far away from them.

Exiting through the back door off the bar's kitchen, she turned right and headed toward the Inner Harbor area. Taking South Broadway again, then on to Eastern Avenue, she crossed over Jones Falls to Pier 6.

She picked up the walking tour path and made her way to Pier 5 on the south end to see the Seven Foot Knoll Lighthouse. Near the Institute of Marine and Environmental Technology, was the U.S. Coast Guard cutter, the U.S.C.G.C. Taney which had been at Pearl Harbor on December 7, 1941, when the Japanese attacked. On the next Pier was a Hard Rock Café and a Barnes and Nobel bookstore, neither of which she cared to explore. Moving on to Pier 3 was the National Aquarium, which to her dismay was closing at eight o'clock, not allowing her enough time to explore the exhibits. There were a couple of other historic ships along the pier, the U.S.S. Cod and the Chesapeake. Celia didn't think she would be able to finish walking around the inner harbor; it was much bigger than she had anticipated, and she was ready to find a restaurant a bit closer to her hotel. She remembered seeing the Rec Pier Chop House across the street from Kooper's and thought she would give it a try.

Picking up her pace, she retraced her steps back to Thames Street. Back on South Broadway, she noticed the two men she had seen earlier. This time, they caught her eye. One began an animated conversation with the other, pulling him along toward her. She lost sight of them in the crowds, and hopefully they couldn't see her either. She ducked into a nearby shop and begged the salesperson to let her out the back way. She was able to skirt around the backs of the shops and find a narrow alley that would put her back on Thames Street. She got to the Chop House and asked the employees manning the outdoor reception and valet area how she could get into the restaurant. They pointed to the door on her left and she ran inside. Out of breath, she found the bathroom to compose herself and freshen up a bit. When she was done, she approached the hostess at the front podium, who led her to a table right in front of the large, plate glass window that overlooked the outdoor reception and Thames Street. Quickly putting on her reading glasses and pulling the oversized menu in front of her face, she was able to observe the street in front of her without fear those men would be able to see her or recognize her.

The waiter came over and asked if she was ready to order.

"May I have a few more minutes? I'm not sure what I want; there are so many good choices But I am ready to order a glass of wine. Do you have a Sauvignon Blanc by the glass?"

"Yes, we do, it is a Honig 2018, very good from Napa" responded the waiter.

"I'll take it and if you could give me a few more minutes I'll be ready to order."

As he left, Celia saw the men walking past on Thames Street, clearly agitated and noticeably looking for someone.

The waiter brought her wine, and she placed her order. About fifteen minutes later her food arrived; grilled swordfish with Salsa Rossa and broccoli rabe. It was wonderful. She had looked at staying at the hotel here, but the room rates were twice as much as the Marriott. She had been able to save a considerable amount of money since Greg had given her an apartment along with her salary, but she didn't feel she should be overly extravagant in her spending, although she did feel she deserved to pamper herself on this trip.

When she finished, she paid her bill and went outside. A taxi was just dropping off a fare, so she got in and requested the driver take her to her hotel. She figured this way, she wouldn't run into those men again and besides, it was very dark and felt it would be much safer than walking alone.

Celia slept in the next morning, waking up at nine thirty. She packed her bags, checked out and got something to eat at the hotel's breakfast buffet. The next leg of her trip, to Fayetteville, North Carolina would only take about six hours, so she wouldn't need to rush.

There was nothing of interest for her to see in Fayetteville; it was just halfway between New Jersey and Tampa, Florida. She had decided to break up the first portion of her trip by stopping in Baltimore, then to Fayetteville. The longest part of her drive would be from Fayetteville to Tampa.

Taking the Capital Beltway to I-95 South, she arrived at her hotel about four thirty in the afternoon. After checking in and going to her room she was disappointed to find there were no towels, toilet paper or facial tissues so she had to return to the front desk to complain. Apparently, there had been a problem with their supplier, but the rooms should be stocked within the next hour or two. The front desk clerk suggested she go to the restaurant next door for their happy hour and dinner. This was the best idea Celia heard all day, so she took the woman's suggestion. When she returned, the requested and expected items had been delivered as promised. Feeling very drowsy after three glasses of wine and a not-so-great dinner, she went to bed.

Celia woke up feeling refreshed and was shocked to see it was five o'clock when she checked her phone. Well, since she was wide awake and having a long drive ahead of her, she quickly packed up her car to leave. No one was at the front desk at that ungodly hour, so she could not formally check out. She assumed they would email her receipt. Seeing a Bojangles Famous Chicken 'n Biscuits across the street, Celia drove over and ordered a biscuit egg and cheese and a large coffee with milk at the drive through window. After receiving her order, she parked in a spot in front of the restaurant to get her food and drink situated before getting back on I-95 South.

As she was doing so, she spotted a car driving under the hotel porte-cochere and two men got out of their car. They each took a side of the hotel and began looking at the parked cars.

Celia immediately recognized these men as the same ones she saw multiple times in Baltimore. She quickly put her coffee in the cup holder and sandwich back in the bag and headed toward the interstate. Panicking now, she drove eighty-five miles per hour with her eyes constantly returning to the rearview mirror.

What is going on she thought? Could this have anything to do with her suspicions at the apartment? Would Greg have her followed or could someone else have a reason to stalk her? Was her ex-husband looking to start trouble again? Greg had been talking to Mike O'Ryan before she left, could he have told Mike where she was heading? Could he have something to do with those missing tenants?

Celia decided she would have to keep her eyes open for those men. Hopefully, she would be able to put many miles between them as she headed to Tampa. She promised herself she would call Miranda once she arrived at Kim's apartment.

With traffic and a few needed rest stops for the bathroom, food and coffee, Celia arrived at Kim's apartment about six o'clock that evening. Once into Florida it had been a very boring drive and Celia had fought to maintain her focus on the road and not drift off to sleep. Tampa, on the other hand, was anything but boring. The highways were loaded with traffic and crazy drivers, both resident and tourist. There was so much adrenaline pumping in her system that she feared she wouldn't be able to get a good night sleep. But as soon as she sat down in Kim's cozy apartment, was handed a glass of white wine, her heart rate began to slow down.

"How can you drive here?" asked Celia. "These people are nuts!"

"Well, you kind of get used to it. You are right though; the drivers are really bad here. I guess that is why my car insurance is so expensive even though I have a great driving record. There are so many uninsured motorists the insurance companies must recoup their losses somehow. Can you imagine if I got a few a tickets or had an accident?" responded Kim.

Pushing her fear about the two men from her mind and her torturous drive into Tampa, Celia began to unwind and enjoy the evening with her daughter. Kim had made shrimp scampi with garlic bread and a tossed salad which Celia found impressive. Her little girl was all grown up, living on her own, taking care of herself and learning how to cook. By the time they decided to go to bed, Celia had completely forgotten about her decision to call Miranda Craig and tell her about the two men.

CHAPTER 29

Mike had been worried when Greg told him Celia was looking through his leasing records and asking questions. Thankfully, he was able to bullshit Greg and appeased him with a report on his services. Of course, the report would only show what Greg wanted to see. It definitely wouldn't show how much money Mike was making on the side, through account transfers and scam phone calls or how many of Greg's tenants had left. Seven wasn't it or was it more? He lost count. Celia somehow was on to him or at least she knew something wasn't right.

Mike had Eddie contact a couple of guys they had used in the past when they needed extra help. Phil Potter and Lester Mancini had been private investigators for years but lost their licenses after performing illegal activities. They were wiretapping, recording conversations, trespassing on private property without the permission of any of the parties. They were able to avoid jail time when they agreed to share the name of the person who hired them, violating their private investigator code of ethics. Clearly, they had no ethics, which was perfect for Mike and what he needed to have done.

Mike and Eddie had never shared their full names nor met Phil and Lester in person. Their communications were strictly over burner phones and money was to be wired to an offshore, numbered account, half up front. Mike shared Celia's name, type of car (they would have to get her plate number if they needed it) and the fact that she was headed to Key West. Greg had let it slip that she would be stopping in Baltimore, specifically Fells Point, then to Fayetteville, North Carolina, and finally Tampa where her daughter Kim lived. The two would be driving to Key West for a few days' vacation. Mike wanted her followed and eliminated. He didn't care how; it just needed to be done quietly and her body not found. And it had to be done before she figured out exactly what Mike and Eddie were up to and contacted the police. Time was of the essence. Phil and Lester assured him it could be done and since she was headed through some remote areas, disposing of her body would be easy, like on Alligator Alley. Once they could get close, they would track her car. If information was relayed to someone else, before they could get rid of her, they would take care of the other person at no extra charge.

It had been two days since Celia left and Mike hadn't heard from Phil or Lester. Every tick of the clock increased the chances Celia might be communicating her concerns to Greg, Miranda Craig or someone else. No one had raised an alarm, so he assumed that concerns were limited to Celia. He was anxious to hear what was happening and if they were successful in catching up to her.

Not able to wait any longer, Mike picked up the burner phone and placed the call. Phil answered the phone but didn't say anything.

"Hey, Phil, it's Mike. I need to know if you found her."

"Mike, I told you we would call after everything was done."

"Yeah, I know" replied Mike. "But I'm paying you a shit ton of money, so I need a daily report."

"Well, I ain't gonna give you dailies, it's not our process," explained Phil, "but I will tell you what we got so far. We were able to spot her in Fells Point but somehow, she saw us and got spooked and did a runner. We looked all over for her but couldn't find her. When she used her credit card for a hotel in Fayetteville, North Carolina, we high-tailed it down there, but when we got there at the crack-o-dawn, she had already left. We've been searching to see where she's staying in the Key's, but her card hasn't been used. We are going to try to catch up with her on I-75 toward Tampa before she gets into the city. Then we can follow her to her destination there and then on to Key West. We're thinking the Everglades on her way down will be a great spot. What do you think?"

"What do I think?" asked Mike. "I think you and Lester are a couple of morons! What did you do that spooked her? Never mind, just get down there. Once you get her, I want you to sweat her and find out what she knows and who she told. Use her kid for leverage if you need to. Get it done!" Mike slammed down the phone after he hit the end button.

CHAPTER 30

Miranda had placed the missing person's report with Detective Morris, providing him with all the information in Karen Sinclair's rental file. She also let him know that she might be hiring an investigator to help look around. She told the detective she wouldn't step on his toes but was just too worried and feared there might be some liability issues. He said he wasn't offended and frankly would welcome any help finding these people. There had been no trace of the other two and he was worried the same would be true for this third one.

Next Miranda knew she had to call John Franklin as soon as possible. He had been so helpful during the summer that she didn't hesitate to pick up her phone again.

"John, it's Miranda."

"Hey, Miranda. What's up?"

"I think I have another situation that requires your aide," said Miranda laughing. "Although, it really isn't funny at all. Consider my laughter a form of hysteria."

"OK…" said John after a moment of hesitation.

"We have had some tenants go missing under suspicious circumstances over the last few months. You remember over the summer I told you we were buying that apartment building in Somerville, New Jersey. Just to recap, Jack and I bought the apartment from a man named Greg Baker. He owns quite a few buildings and complexes in this area. He sold this one because it was just one building and he wanted to focus his investments in larger, multiple building complexes."

"Shortly after we closed on the building the apartment manager, Celia, who we agreed would stay on for a while, called me and said one of the tenants seemed to have died."

"What do you mean, 'seemed to have died?'" asked John.

"When the tenant's friend had come to check up on him," Miranda continued, "he found him apparently dead on the floor and had to go outside for his phone since there was no phone in the apartment he could find and called for help. When he returned the friend was gone. Later, he received an email from the friend saying he was sorry, he hadn't been happy at the new place, then signed it Al, which was out of character according to the friend."

"Celia called the police, but they couldn't find any indication that he had been killed and with the email saying he was alright, declined to pursue it further until some other evidence proved otherwise."

"Then another tenant, a female, went missing but because of an email she had written to her boyfriend, the police took him into custody after finding her funds had been transferred out of her account to an unknown location and that she had accused him of the theft. She has not been located, either."

"Finally, another woman went missing from our building, which I just reported to the police. Celia has been looking through the leasing records of our property and also checking Greg Baker's other holdings to see if he too has some issues concerning his properties. She had to stop her search when he came in. She has some suspicions as to who might be involved but I would rather have an independent investigation take place. If it leads to this person, then good. Also, tenants have been complaining about crazy phone calls. Celia says they cover a full range of scams and she's worried about our elderly residents. She is out of town in Tampa and Key West with her daughter on a vacation. I thought maybe you could check in with Detective Morris of the Somerville Police about our missing tenants and help me hire someone to do a little digging. All these missing people can't be a coincidence can it? Something is just not right."

"I guess I can do that. So, is it just those three?" asked John.

"We have three that we know of. Greg had one tenant that appeared to wander off and Celia was starting to research if there were others."

"By any chance do you have any vacant apartments right now?" John asked. "I have an idea."

"Yes, we have Karen Sinclair's, which can be ready in a few days. Why?"

"Well, I know a guy who used to work for a big tech firm in San Francisco. The company focused on cyber security, did some defense work and he even helped to recover crypto currency after a ransomware attack on a company. He has been semi-retired and spends his time going after hackers and scammers. I wish I had thought of him this past summer; we could have used him to solve those Long Beach Island spyware issues much quicker. What he does is not exactly legal, and I will have to see if he is willing to employ a little subterfuge by taking on a fake name, fake credentials, disguise, and living in one of your apartments. The guy is pretty well off, so he probably won't charge you, but you will have to give him the apartment gratis."

"That won't be a problem, especially if he can track down the tenants and who is doing this," said Miranda. "How fast do you think you can reach him and convince him to do it?"

"Oh, it should only take a day or two. I think these circumstances will be enough of a carrot that he would jump on it. I'm going to call Detective Morris to see if we can get a look at the electronics and financial stuff that are available for these tenants. Anything else he needs; he will just have to work his secret magic. You didn't hear me say that."

"O…k" Miranda said reluctantly. "Jack and I won't get in trouble, will we?"

"I don't think so. I will just make sure we are out of the loop-plausible deniability. He will work independently then he will disappear. He is not the kind of guy that needs to take a bow."

"I am heading to South Carolina for a wedding so I will need to get him set up in an apartment before I go."

John made some notes to himself on a pad of paper then said, "OK, I will keep in touch and let you know as soon as he says yes. On second thought, don't do anything to Karen Sinclair's apartment. We will have him move in without telling anyone. It will be interesting to see if anyone comes knocking on the door or makes contact with him."

CHAPTER 31

Miranda had had a busy fall; the Chowderfest in the later part of September, then to Napa in mid-October. Her cousin's son, which would make him her first cousin once removed, was getting married the Sunday after Thanksgiving, so Miranda was flying down to Greenville, South Carolina that Saturday. She planned to spend a few days with her relatives while Jack stayed home with their dog Maynard and give help to John, if needed. He had to work Monday and didn't want to fly home late that Sunday night, so she was going without him. Erica, their daughter, decided to spend Thanksgiving with some friends from college and Kevin was still in London for his internship, leaving Miranda free to attend the wedding and not feel guilty. They had plans to spend the entire Christmas holiday break at their shore house on Long Beach Island.

Miranda had finished laying out all her clothes, shoes and cosmetics for her trip when John called to tell her his guy would be at her leasing office that morning at eleven. He would tell her he was looking for a quiet, one bedroom.

Miranda finished her packing and set her suitcases by the garage door for tomorrow morning's flight then rushed to the apartment building where a man was standing by the entrance door. As she approached, he opened the door for her to enter.

"May I help you?" asked Miranda.

"Yes, I'm looking for a quiet, one bedroom apartment. It doesn't matter what floor it's on or if it has a view. It just needs to be quiet."

"Of course," replied Miranda. "I will just get the key and take you right up."

Miranda took the man up the back staircase to the third floor, unlocked the door and handed him the key. "I have had the utilities turned back on, including the internet in the complex's name. If you need anything else, ask John and he will be able to get it for you right away. Thank you for doing this."

"Doing what," said the man.

"Exactly" said Miranda.

When Miranda returned to the office, Mike was standing outside.

"Hey, need some help? New tenant?" Mike asked.

"Hey Mike, no I'm good." Miranda decided to just leave it at that; to say no more. She quickly got her purse and left.

As soon as Miranda left, Mike called Eddie to tell him to check out the new guy.

CHAPTER 32

Key West, Florida

Wanting to get an early start to reach Key West at a decent hour, Kim and Celia went outside to load up Celia's car. Just as they approached the vehicle, Kim said, "Mom, I really hate your car and the seats are not all that comfortable. Why don't we take mine, plus I already have a full tank of gas? That will save us a few minutes and we can be on our way a bit quicker. Your car will be safe here. As you experienced last night, I had to buzz you into the complex. I sent management an email this morning with your car make, model and license plate number so they won't tow you. Guests are allowed to leave their cars here, but management has to be notified."

Celia agreed and they put their suitcases and snacks for the road into Kim's Ford Escape. Celia made sure her old Toyota Camry was locked and in a safe parking space.

After her long drive yesterday, Celia was uncertain if she could tolerate the eight-hour drive to their hotel in the Keys. Thankfully, Kim was eager to drive and let Celia play navigator for the first few hours. The plan was to take 75 South to about Naples, then head east to pick up 95 South through Miami until reaching Route 1, which would take them through to the Keys.

The Overseas Highway was remarkable with forty-two bridges connecting the islands from Miami to Key West at the end. The most incredible bridge was the Seven Mile Bridge at Marathon Key. Prior to reaching Marathon, which was the halfway point, they decided to stop for lunch at Snook's Bayside Restaurant and Tiki Bar in Key Largo. Kim had googled recommendations for lunch in Key Largo and this place was highly endorsed.

When they saw the old, paint chipped sign and the dirt road, they thought those people had been crazy, but after going down the road, it opened up to a beautiful restaurant on the water. Their server suggested the mahi sandwich platter and boy were they glad they took her advice. They had never eaten any fish sandwich so good or so fresh.

They made it into Key West about seven-thirty that night after a long afternoon of traffic, twenty-five mile an hour speed limits and bumper to bumper cars. A valet was waiting for them as they pulled into the parking area of the Crown Plaza Key West La Concha Hotel on Duval Street. He unloaded their suitcases and showed them into the reception desk. After they checked in and cleaned up, got their complimentary drink, dinner was next on the agenda. Kim had done her homework, selecting many of the restaurants they would try while on vacation. The first one she chose was the Rooftop Café.

One of the remarkable things about Key West was that you could park your car and not see it again until you left. The hotel was centrally located so nothing was more than a fifteen or twenty minute walk away.

Mallory Square was nearby. Celia had heard so much about the area where street performers gathered and did their thing at sunset, but it was too late to watch the activities that night. They found the restaurant on Front Street and took the stairs up to the second floor. The hostess sat them at an outdoor table on the balcony overlooking the street where they could see throngs of tourists going in and out of the various shops and restaurants. It was just warm enough to make it bearable to sit outside.

So far Celia could not complain about the quality of food she had been eating, other than at the chain restaurant in Fayetteville. Tonight, she chose a Sonoma white wine, mixed greens with beets, mangos, candied walnuts and blue cheese and Kim ordered a rum punch and a Caesar salad. They split orders of conch fritters and lobster gnocchi. The ladies were exhausted from their trip, stuffed from their meal and decided just to walk back to the hotel and get a good night's sleep.

CHAPTER 33

That same day, Phil and Lester got up and had a nice, leisurely breakfast at their hotel in Tampa, Florida. The tracking device on Celia's car showed she was still at the daughter's apartment. Phil and Lester had spotted Celia on the highway before taking an exit ramp into the city. Maintaining a safe distance so they would not be spotted, they were able to follow her to what they assumed was her daughter's apartment complex. Realizing they wouldn't be able to enter the grounds without a card key or someone's permission, they decided to get a hotel nearby. After dark, they came back, jumped the wall surrounding the complex, found Celia's car and installed the tracker under the chassis. The next morning, they checked out of the hotel, parked near the complex's only exit and waited for them to leave. They thought this would give them the best opportunity to follow and take them out when they neared Everglades State Park. After an entire day of waiting, Phil began to get nervous and suspected they took another car. He had Lester phone one of his contacts to run a motor vehicle search for Kim Ravenscroft. When nothing came up, they decided to just high tail it to Key West to try to find them there.

CHAPTER 34

Thanksgiving Day morning, Celia and Kim decided to walk about a half mile to Harpoon Harry's for breakfast. The bright pink exterior of the building welcomed them inside to a further explosion of color. The walls were decorated with signs and musical instruments. Tiffany style lights hung brightly above the wooden tables. Perusing the menu, they decided on poached eggs, potatoes, toast and coffee. Afterwards, they strolled around the Wharf pier to Mallory Square, vowing to come back later to watch the sun set and enjoy the show put on by the street performers.

By lunch time, much to their dismay, it was raining. A few tourists had umbrellas and others, like themselves, just ran and laughed through the rain. Near the marina, they spotted Conch Republic Seafood. Kim noticed the great view of the boats bobbing in the marina swells. Grabbing a hand full of napkins as they sat down at a table by a window and wiped the rain from their faces and arms. In no time, the waitress brought them their mahi sandwiches, French fries, and Key lime coladas. It was a nice spot to people watch, listen to the seabirds and wait out the rain.

Kim told Celia more about her classes at school, campus activities and the problems she was having with her roommate Beth. Still fuming how Beth had left her high and dry with the hotel bill, Kim did however admit that she was really glad Celia was able to come instead. "Frankly, Mom, I hope she continues to see this guy. She is never around so I have the apartment all to myself. It is so quiet I get a lot of studying done and don't have to schlep all my books and laptop to the library."

On their way to dinner later that night, it began to pour again, raining much harder than it had during the day. Hopping from awning to awning of the stores and businesses along the way, they were able to avoid getting soaked again. However, when they arrived at the restaurant, the front walkway was flooded under a foot of water. Celia had to remove her black suede loafers, wade through the water and splash up the steps leading into the restaurant.

The Grand Café was an old, refurbished house, with modern artwork adorning the walls. It was a strange dichotomy, but it seemed to work. After their bottle of wine arrived and they had their first few sips, Celia began to unwind and really enjoy herself. This is just what she needed, spending time with her wonderful daughter on a warm, but wet island in the middle of nowhere.

Looking over the menu, Celia decided to start with a beet salad and have the spicy mussels as her dinner entrée. Kim ordered the linguini with clams and mussels nestled in a spicy tomato sauce. All the travel had caught up with both of them, or it was the full bottle of wine they drank with dinner, so they decided to head back to the hotel and watch a little TV before falling asleep. Tomorrow would be another day of walking around, a bit of shopping and of course eating wonderful food.

Friday morning, they were up early and decided that they wanted to go back to Harpoon Harry's. It was such a fun little place, and the service was fantastic. Celia decided on the French Toast with bananas and Kim selected biscuits and gravy. Heading in the opposite direction from the previous day, they chose to walk down Duval Street all the way to the other end of the island. When they were almost through town, they stopped at Southern Most Smoothie and split a mixture of Key lime, orange juice and mango. It was so refreshing.

They continued south looking through some of the stores along the way and marveled at the art galleries filled with beautiful paintings of roosters. Roosters were everywhere- ceramic, painted and live. Roosters and chickens roamed freely along the streets at their feet, between buildings and in the flower beds of homes.

Finally, when they reached the end of the sidewalk, tourists surrounded a large bullet shaped landmark. The top part was bright red, then striped black, gold, red and black at the base. In the upper most red section was a triangle of yellow and blue denoting 'The Conch Republic.' In the remaining sections it read: *90 miles to Cuba. Southernmost point Continental USA, Key West Florida.* Celia hadn't realized the United States was that close to Cuba or that this landmark symbolized the bottom edge of the country.

When they got back into town it was nearly lunch time. A sign for Pinchers Key West hung from a balcony above enticing them to eat Florida seafood. Initially, they thought they would like to sit out on the balcony, but it was so windy they asked to be moved inside. Walls were adorned with festive signs: "It's Always Christmas in Key West;" "Palm Trees Make Great Christmas Trees;" and "Drink Beer, Be Happy." Kim loved her mahi, so she got a sandwich with fries and Celia decided to try the grilled shrimp, coleslaw and applesauce. Simplistic, yet so delicious and they washed it down with two buckets of rum and diet cokes. Celia couldn't help but laugh and said to Kim, "This reminds me of college adventures with my best friend Jayne."

With lunch and rum buckets finished, they opened the door to leave the restaurant and were greeted with a hard rain, driving directly in their faces. Celia slammed the door closed, turned around and yelled to the bar maid, "Two more buckets if you please!" They returned to their previous table and Celia pulled out the deck of playing cards she always carried with her. They played Rummy and drank rum for an hour and a half until the rain stopped. The two ladies strolled back to the hotel, took a nap in an attempt to sleep off the rum from lunch, then showered before dinner.

Celia was relieved the day had been uneventful. She had been able to focus on her daughter and not her concerns about the missing tenants. Kim had been searching the internet for dinner ideas and decided she wanted to try the Thirsty Mermaid. It was a cute little place off the beaten path. The service was a bit slow, but like most restaurants in Florida the fish was caught locally each day. Celia had a Sauvignon Blanc to start with short rib gnocchi and Kim had yellow tail snapper. The order got mixed up by the kitchen forcing Kim to wait on her food while Celia's meal was being served. They were not pleased but realized that all restaurants had off nights especially like in the Conch Republic.

The long nap help Celia feel refreshed and ready for the evening. On Duval Street, downtown Key West, sat Sloppy Joe's Bar, an historic treasure that opened in 1933 on the day Prohibition ended. It was originally known as the Blind Pig, later to be renamed the Silver Slipper, then finally Sloppy Joe's because the floor was always wet with ice. It was a favorite Hemingway haunt and finally moved to its present location just across the street in 1937.

Even though there was a huge crowd, they surmised because of the holiday weekend, they were somehow able to get a table. The band was loud and animated, having long and funny conversations with the patrons. Celia wasn't sure if she was laughing at the band's jokes, the fact that her feet were sticking to the floor, or that she was quite drunk. She was glad she could turn things around for Kim and they were able to spend this time together. They both needed it.

When they realized they had had enough to drink, especially after all the drinking they had done that day, they settled up the tab and exited the bar. Celia noticed two men entering from the side door as they were leaving from the front. A feeling of unease settled over her. She was positive these were the same men who had been following her. Ducking her head to conceal her face, she grabbed Kim's arm and led her out onto the sidewalk.

"Kim, I really have to go to the bathroom, but I don't want to use the grungy one in the bar. Mind if we sprint back to the hotel?" On the run back to the hotel Celia kept looking over her shoulder, certain the men would be following.

Celia tossed and turned all night. She couldn't get her mind off those men and what they might want. More convinced than ever that they were looking for her, but couldn't understand why, or what she could do about it? Her number one priority was to keep Kim safe and the minute she was sure they were the target; she would get Kim out of Key West.

CHAPTER 35

Deciding a new breakfast location was in order Saturday morning, Kim pulled out her phone and started an internet search. Two Friends Patio Restaurant, which Trip Advisor rated highly, would be their next stop. As they walked, Kim proceeded to read off fun facts about the joint: it used to be a saloon, has live music every day, had the first woman bartender, housed a bordello in the upper floor, just to name a few. The live entertainment in the bar area was already in session, and it was beginning to get crowded when they arrived. The two asked to be seated at the opposite end of the restaurant from where the music was being played. Hopefully, it wouldn't be too loud thus allowing conversation without shouting. They ordered poached eggs, toast, biscuits and potatoes- lots of starch to soak up all the alcohol from the day and night before. Thankfully, the patio was enclosed, with the plastic side panels down, as it was starting to rain yet again. Celia noted that there were dozens of chickens and roosters wandering around the floor by their feet. It was so strange, yet so fun. She also wondered how the local health department dealt with the filth left by the fowl.

Across the street a colorful kiosk sat in the middle of the sidewalk advertising the Conch Tour Train. The train was an outing that led people all around Key West, giving visitors a history lesson about the area. The conductors were knowledgeable and included fun, interesting facts about the Keys. Thirty dollars apiece was a bit hefty, but Celia thought it would be fun, educational and it would give them an idea of where they might want to spend more time or go to dinner that night. The rain had finally stopped, and the sun was coming out; it was turning out to be a nice morning.

The Conch Train was definitely a touristy thing to do but as the ride went on, both she and Kim learned so much about Key West. The driver talked about the history of piracy in the waters, salt production for food preservation and the ownership of the land. One of the first lucrative businesses in the Keys was salvaging the wrecked ships which foundered on the Florida reefs. Next came the sponge industry and then the influence of Cuban people, who came to work at the Key West cigar factories. Most fled after Castro took over the island. Following construction of the lighthouses and installation of navigational beacons, the salvage industry began to decline.

As the train passed by the Ernest Hemingway Home and Museum at 907 Whitehead, the conductor told the group about the island's most famous resident and his love of cats. In the 1930s, Hemingway received a gift of a polydactyl cat (one with six toes) from a sea captain, which he added to his many other cats. Even now, the forty to fifty cats still at the museum either have six toes or carry the trait.

The most interesting dialogue, in Celia's opinion, explained the presence of the chickens and the roosters. Apparently, the Cubans brought the fowl with them. As was their custom, cock fighting was their premier sport, but the Key West officials and residents did not agree with the activity. Cock fighting was eventually banned, and the Cubans retaliated by releasing all their chickens and roosters to the streets of Key West. Now, it was a finable offense to kill any of the birds. When their numbers got too high, they were trapped and relocated to a wildlife center.

When the tour was nearing its end, Celia again spotted the two men walking around an arts and crafts show set up on a side street. As her train went by, she ducked down in her seat to avoid being seen but was still able to keep an eye on them. They were scanning the crowd that was mingling around the tents, then gave a cursory glance to the train passing by. Having felt a brief sense of relief earlier, Celia now felt a new wave of panic. They were on the prowl and with Key West being a rather small area, Celia realized it would only be a matter of time before they found her. The thought of prematurely ending Kim's vacation soured her stomach. Maintaining a constant vigilance was her only option.

The conductor had mentioned Caroline's Cafe during his talk, so they decided to head back to Duval Street for lunch after the tour was over. The outdoor tables were hidden to the street by a bar and patio umbrellas. Celia chose a table near the back with a clear view of the main street entrance, seeing why this was a favorite place for people watching patrons.

"Kim, I think we move from one meal to the next here, with only a little bit of activity and a lot of drinking in between," joked Celia as they sat down.

"Yeah, that's the thing about a vacation like this. There really aren't any sunbathing beaches and the weather has been a bit cold and rainy. But, hey, I'm not complaining. I have never had such great food. But then I only have the slop they feed us at school to compare it to."

Looking at the menu and then turning to the server, Celia said, "I'm going to have the shrimp wrap with bibb lettuce, chopped cucumber, shredded carrots, rice noodles, and the soy peanut sauce, and to drink I think I will try your Pinot Grigio."

The server turned to Kim, who ordered the grilled yellowfin tuna on a bed of greens and a Mojito. As their food came out, the sun began to shine bringing with it a wonderful warmth and feeling of wellbeing. But would that feeling last?

CHAPTER 36

Mike O'Ryan had not received any information from Jerry and Phil on their progress to eliminate Celia Ravenscroft. He had insisted that they be quick and careful, and they had insisted that he should not phone them for updates, assuring him he would know when the job was done. Of course, he didn't want to be connected with their actions if they succeeded in killing Celia, so Mike had finally agreed to stop calling them. Mike had instructed Eddie when setting up the hit on Celia, the men would only know their first names. He knew this would not be a problem for them, the only information Jerry and Phil needed was the name of the intended victim and how they would receive their money.

Initially, they all used burner phones to make the arrangements and the down payment was to be wired to an offshore account. Phil and Jerry desperately needed cash because with the loss of their private investigator licenses came the loss of any legitimate clients. Therefore, a new plan was worked out to receive the down payment. Cash would be left in a remote location in Warren, a nearby town. Mike had insisted he make the drop, not fully trusting Eddie with such a hefty sum of money and a critical hit, getting rid of Celia Ravenscroft.

Phil had sent him a text to drop the money in the trash can outside of the first fenced in area of the dog run at the East County Park. Mike had been to Warren several times, eating dinner at a few of the restaurants near the town center. After checking the Somerset County Park Commission website for directions, he headed off in the late afternoon hoping it wasn't too busy there. It had been a bit cold and spitting rain, so he doubted anyone would want to hang out in the park.

He turned right off Reinman Road into the park entrance and immediately noticed the parking lot was empty. Retrieving the bag of cash from his car trunk, he proceeded to the trail on the right that led down a hill toward a circular path around a pond. As he continued to walk, he saw the fenced-in dog area up on the next hill.

Looking around for any sign of life, his first thought was, this would be an ideal place to hide a body. There was no one around, lots of trees, dense ground cover, numerous hiding places and escape routes. To his far left he could barely make out the Warren Middle School and football field and various maintenance sheds. To his right, just up past the dog park were two soccer fields, parking lots and more trees. He would have to file away this location should he ever need a secluded dump site if Eddie's funeral home contact was not able to come through.

He spotted the trash can up ahead and did a slow three hundred sixty degree turn to make sure no one was around. The money bag was not too large, about the size of a woman's pocketbook and it fit nicely into the trash can. He was to text Phil when the drop was complete. He was hopeful they would be successful; they had come highly recommended.

It had been well over a week since Celia left on her vacation and there had been no news. He had searched the internet for any deaths reported along the highway south, in Tampa, the Everglades or Key West. Mike had even asked Greg if Celia was having fun with her daughter, but Greg just shrugged and said he was giving her a lot of space and frankly he was too busy with his new real estate deal to be playing phone tag with her. She had told him she would call when she was on her way home and since she hadn't called, he assumed she was still with Kim in Florida. Then he looked at Mike and asked if there was a problem with the apartment building. Mike just said, "No problem, I was just curious."

Before he could walk away, Greg turned to him and said, "Hey, I've been looking at those reports you prepared for me when Celia left. I left you a number of messages about taking an hour to go over them. I have a few questions. I don't know if it's me or you need to work on your math or spreadsheet skills, but I found some discrepancies I want to go over and see if we can figure out what the problem is. Are you free tomorrow or the next day?"

"Sure Greg, either day is fine, let me check my calendar and call you later with a suitable time." Mike hurried away before Greg could say another word.

The next day, Mike spotted a Sheriff's investigator walking around talking with several residents of the Craig's apartment building. Mike overheard some of the questions being asked. Most dealt with how they found out about this apartment building, any concerns they had living there and did they know the three tenants who recently left. He quickly ducked out of sight before the investigator saw him.

Rushing to his car in the parking lot, Mike pulled out his phone and called Eddie. "Hey, Eddie, I need your help right away. We have to take matters into our own hands. I just saw cops at the apartment asking questions. First, I want you to go to the drug store and buy four or five large bottles of eye drops, you know, the ones that have tetrahydrozoline in them. Then I want you to go to Greg's office and grab his eye drops from the bathroom making sure to leave his prints on the bottle, so take some latex gloves with you. I know he has at least one bottle, he is always using the drops because of all the computer work he does."

"After you have done that, I want you to break into Celia and Greg's apartment and put as much of the eye drops as you can in all the liquids they have in their refrigerator. Leave one bottle, wiping off your prints and throw it in the trash can in her kitchen and leave the bottle with Greg's prints on it on the kitchen counter." Mike had recently seen a murder mystery on television where eye drops were used to kill someone, with symptoms mimicking a heart attack. He also remembered a story of a South Carolina woman who had poisoned and murdered her husband by putting doses of eye drops in his food over a number of days. Mike hoped this killing method was farfetched enough that the medical examiner wouldn't test for it and just assume that Greg died of heart failure being the driven, ambitious, businessman that he was.

The eye drops were soluble in water and unnoticeable, and he also knew quite a few men used them as a date rape drug and no prescription was needed!

CHAPTER 37

Greg had been reviewing Mike's report for the third time; still not certain what the numbers were showing. Did he really have that many people leaving prior to lease expirations? He went to his computer and pulled up the lease tracking program. Over the years, he had had a number of people leave early, but these current numbers seem to be quite high.

Was Mike somehow churning, like brokers who trade excessively, by getting people to leave simply to earn another fee when a new person moved in?

He pulled out his cell phone and called Celia. This discussion with Mike reminded him how much he relied on her opinion, and he missed seeing and talking with her on a daily basis. She should be on her way back to New Jersey about now and he really needed to talk with her about these numbers. Her phone went to voicemail, so he left her a brief message.

"Hey Celia, I hope your vacation was fantastic with Kim. Please give me a call when you get a chance, I would like to go over the report Mike gave me. I have some issues with his numbers and would like to know what you think. I will be going back to the apartment shortly to clean up then I have a meeting at the bank with Roger. You can reach me on my cell at any time. I am going to meet with Mike tomorrow or the next day and would appreciate your feedback. I can't wait to see you; I have really missed you!"

Greg got back to the apartment about an hour later, walked into the kitchen and pulled out a water bottle from the refrigerator. He downed about three quarters of the bottle and headed to the bathroom for a shower. He quickly dressed, finished the water and noticed that he was feeling a bit nauseous. Thinking it was probably dehydration, he went to the kitchen and grabbed another bottle to drink while on his way to the bank.

Running a bit late, he was thankful the bank was only a few blocks from the apartment. He was still feeling a bit unsteady as he walked into the bank's main entrance and was now wondering if he was getting the flu. It was that time of year and he had forgotten to get his annual flu shot. His first thought was, 'Oh great, I get sick when Celia is coming back. That's not the homecoming I was planning.'

Greg was shown into the conference room and asked to wait until Roger Stanton, the bank manager, finished his phone call. The purpose of the meeting was to discuss financing options for a new building he planned to purchase. Feeling nervous because this would be his biggest loan ever, he chugged the rest of the water.

Ten minutes later when Roger entered the conference room, he found Greg lying on the floor unconscious. He rushed to the table and picked up the phone to call 911. As instructed, he moved Greg onto his side and made sure there was nothing obstructing his airway. Greg appeared to be breathing so there was nothing to be done until help showed up. Roger's assistant showed the paramedics to the conference room as soon as they arrived. Bank personnel huddled around outside of the conference room as they watched with amazement at how in control the EMT's were, checking vitals, starting an intravenous line and fluids, all the while communicating with the local hospital. With these preliminaries complete, and Greg on the stretcher, they wheeled him out to the van telling Roger they were taking him to Robert Wood Johnson University Hospital in Somerville.

CHAPTER 38

Phil and Lester had been scouring the streets of Key West all day searching for signs of Celia and her daughter. The men thought they caught a glimpse of the women on the tourist train but were unable to catch up to them. All they could do was to separate, Phil on one end of town and Lester on the other.

After receiving confirmation from Eddie that Greg had been taken to the hospital and his condition was dire but not dead, Mike decided it was time to take Draconian measures to prevent discovery and capture by the authorities. He knew with the police snooping around, Celia and Greg still alive, it would only be a matter of time. He had not heard from the two bungling thugs which could only mean one thing. They had not completed the job.

He pulled out his cell phone and placed the call.

As soon as Phil picked up the phone, Mike shouted, "What the hell is going on down there?"

"Hey, don't worry! We have it covered. They are still down here I'm sure, it won't be long until we know where they are staying, and we do what we were sent here to do."

"I don't think so. I am sending my guy down there tonight. I will text you his flight information so you can pick him up from the airport. We need his eyes down there. Things are really hot up here now and we need to move out." Mike hung up without another word. He was seething mad and beginning to panic.

Searching through the Expedia website, he found a direct Delta flight from LaGuardia that would get Eddie to Key West by around five thirty that night. He booked and charged one ticket, called Eddie with the details and texted the times and gate information to Phil. Eddie did not need to pack a bag, no clothes were needed, they had work to do. On the flight down, Eddie would strategize how to find Celia, get rid of the investigators and then leave the country until things cooled down. Lester and Phil, he was sure, had weapons so he wouldn't have to reach out to his contacts in South Florida.

Keslie Patch-Bohrod

CHAPTER 39

It had been a long, balmy day of walking through the city. Celia was exhausted and frightened for their safety. Mother and daughter decided to go back to the Roof Top Café. Dinner had been fantastic the first night so it was fitting they would finish their vacation food fest there. Since it was about a fifteen minute walk from their hotel, Celia had to keep a sharp eye, even though the sidewalks were crowded with tourists, in the case those men were out and about looking for her.

Kim ordered an iced tea to start, saying she was saving herself until they went to Irish Kevin's Bar later on Duval Street. They had seen the bar earlier on their Conch Train tour and decided they would give it a try after dinner. It too, was a favorite local bar that offered live music, food and drinks.

Celia ordered a Vesper, reciting James Bond's ingredients: three parts Gordon's gin, one part vodka, half part Kina Lillet and lemon peel. The server returned with Kim's iced tea but told Celia they didn't have Kina Lillet, but just a regular lillet. Celia said that was fine. "Oh wait, please also add a splash of St. Germaine to the mixture and hold the fruit." She giggled to herself adding in the Felix Leiter line from the movie. The server just gave her a funny look, not understanding the reference to the lemon peel.

The waiter returned with a beautiful long stemmed Martini glass, Celia, taking a sip of the very cold cocktail said, "Wonderful! We are ready to place our dinner order. We would like one Key West Conch Chowder, one lobster and gnocchi with corn, spinach and black truffle cream and one Pasta Basilico with fresh basil, plum tomatoes, garlic and olive oil over linguini."

Their meal was just as good as their first night. If they ever returned to Key West, they would definitely eat here again.

Irish Kevin's was crowded by the time Celia and Kim arrived. They walked around from table to table for a while looking for two seats, as a lone performer sang and played guitar. It was similar to Sloppy Joe's in that it was a classic dive bar; shoes stuck to the floor when you walked, the tables were sticky from spilt beer and people were packed in like sardines. Finally, a group of people left a table along the side of the club near the bathrooms, and they were able to sit down and order drinks. A family came in and asked if they could join them and they struck up a conversation. Celia, however, was not paying attention to the conversation as she was intent on scanning the crowd, worried that the two men she spotted earlier in the day might come into the bar. She still couldn't believe they were looking for her and her anxiety level grew at the prospects of them finding her. It was too much of a coincidence that they kept popping up.

Moments later she noticed familiar figures walk into the bar, stop by the hostess podium and look around. They moved off to the back of the bar by the singer, glancing around as they cut through the crowd then ended up standing by the stage. As one of the men turned around, scanning the crowd, all of the air left Celia's lungs. She recognized the man, and it wasn't good. It was Eddie the thug that hung out with Mike.

As the men headed for the opposite end of the room, Celia saw this as her chance to get away without them noticing her, so she grabbed Kim by the arm and pulled her out of the bar. They ran down the sidewalk until they made it to Sloppy Joe's. All the while, Kim was yelling at her "What is going on? Why did we leave so fast? I was having a good time talking with those people! Are you nuts?"

They found a dark corner in the upper left-hand part of the bar near the stage. Celia could monitor all the entrances, of which there were many, plus they were close to the restrooms if they had to hide in a hurry. They were also near an exit should they have to leave quickly. They ordered two mojitos and began to listen to the band.

When the band went on a break, Celia took the opportunity to finally explain the situation to her daughter. "Kim, I was hoping that I was crazy or just paranoid, but there have been two men following me since I left New Jersey. I first saw them on the street in Fells Point when I stopped in Baltimore, then they hung around the bar and restaurant where I stopped for a drink then dinner. I saw them at my hotel in Fayetteville, North Carolina extremely early in the morning and finally several times here in Key West. I am not sure what is going on, but I also just saw a man that works for Mike O'Ryan which now makes me certain they have been looking for me. I suspected Mike O'Ryan had something to do with several of my tenants disappearing under what I consider mysterious circumstances. I think it would be wise to leave tomorrow right after breakfast, because driving at night would scare me more. We wouldn't see them coming."

They decided to stay at Sloppy Joe's until almost midnight, keeping an eye on the crowd to make sure the men had not come in. When they finally headed back to the hotel, they attempted to disguise themselves. Celia took the scarf she from her neck and wrapped it around her hair. Kim pulled up her hood on her jacket. They kept looking around them as they headed back to the hotel.

Up early Sunday morning, they packed their suitcases, retrieved their car from the valet and drove to breakfast at Harpoon Harry's. Celia's last breakfast in Key West was a traditional eggs Benedict and coffee and Kim ordered biscuits and sausage gravy. As soon as they were finished eating, they paid their bill, walked across the street and got into their car.

When Phil and Lester retrieved Eddie from the airport the night before, Eddie announced that he had a plan. They would check out the obvious night spots in a last-ditch attempt to find Celia in town. If that failed, he told them the women would eventually have to leave Key West and to their advantage, there was only one road out. They would park at mile marker eight near the Key West Naval Air Station and wait for the women to drive by, and then follow them up Route 1. They would each take turns watching for a car with the women, to insure they didn't miss them even if they left in the middle of the night. It could be a long wait and slow going once they spotted them, but at least they would be assured of not missing them.

Keslie Patch-Bohrod

CHAPTER 40

Abbeville, South Carolina

The trip for the wedding was to be short, with Miranda flying down to Greenville, South Carolina that Saturday, the ceremony on Sunday and then spend a few days with her relatives.

Miranda was excited to see her cousin Matt and his family. She hadn't seen them for years and they had recently purchased a huge property in Abbeville that everyone said was quite impressive.

Waking up at five fifteen in the morning on that Saturday in a fog, Miranda picked up her cell phone from beside the bed to turn off the alarm. She would need to hustle this morning, get dressed, finish packing, feed Maynard and make a bagel for her flight to Greenville.

Jack was up doing his thing, packing his briefcase and eating his breakfast. He figured he would get in a few hours' work after dropping Miranda off at the airport.

Thankfully, the traffic was light, and she was able to update Jack on John's proposed activities. They arrived at the United Terminal C just after six thirty a.m. Miranda checked in at the kiosk for her boarding pass and rushed to the TSA pre-check line where she found out her flight was located in Terminal A. Ugh!

Luck would have it, after placing her bags on the screening belt and moving through the body scanner, she was randomly selected for additional screening. Thankfully, the process only took an additional couple of minutes. The agent took her iPhone and iPad, swabbed it with a special cloth, found nothing out of the ordinary and released her to continue toward her gate. Miranda asked for instructions to get to Terminal A and was told there was a shuttle bus just off the C71 gate that would take her there. The bus was waiting when she walked through the corridor. She boarded and rolled to terminal A. Phew! Made it to the gate with time to spare.

Miranda's flight was uneventful and arrived at the Greenville Spartanburg International Airport on time. Even though it was listed as the second busiest airport in the state, Miranda was able to grab her bag, pick up her rental car at Alamo and get to her hotel in downtown Greenville in under an hour.

Many of her family members were already at the hotel, so she spent the rest of the afternoon catching up with everyone in the lobby bar. Dinner that night would be in a local restaurant that was a short walk up the hill into town so no one would have to worry about drinking and driving after a having a few more drinks.

Sunday, during the wedding, Miranda got a text from Celia saying she was leaving Key West and would be back in Tampa that night. She desperately needed to talk with Miranda about the apartment building and she suspected something illegal was going on. She was certain she was being followed and had even seen Eddie from O'Ryan Real Estate Placement Services.

As soon as the ceremony was over, Miranda left the church to call Celia for more details.

"Hi, Celia. I have a few minutes to chat before we move on to the wedding reception. Do you think you are still being followed?"

"Miranda, Kim and I are about halfway back to Tampa. I have not seen anyone since last night, but I just know they must be out there. I saw them in Baltimore, Fayetteville and Key West. I am going to have Kim pack a few things when we get back to her place and stay at a friend's apartment until we get things sorted out. I don't want these men finding Kim. Once she's settled, I will start the drive back to New Jersey stopping only when necessary and in crowded places."

Miranda told her she had contacted a friend of hers that might be able to help or at least provide some advice. He was John Franklin, an ex-secret service agent and currently employed in a New Jersey Sheriff's office. He had been extremely helpful over the past summer when Miranda uncovered a Russian spy, who had been breaking into homes in Loveladies and installing spyware. She had alerted John that something might be wrong at their apartment building. He had suggested putting someone in an apartment to investigate the disappearances and phone calls.

After the wedding ceremony and reception, Miranda returned to the hotel where more activities were planned in the bar. She went to her room to phone John.

"Hey, John, it's Miranda."

"Hi Miranda. I was going to call you later tonight. Jack thought you would be available between eight and nine."

"Did you find out anything?" asked Miranda.

"Yes, I have quite a bit to tell you," responded John.

"Great, but first I need to conference in Celia, our property manager. Let me see if I can reach her." Miranda hit a few buttons on her phone and luckily Celia was available to be part of the conversation.

"Celia, why don't you tell John about these men" suggest Miranda.

"There isn't too much I can tell you," began Celia. "There are two men, average I guess you'd call them, and they seem to keep popping up wherever I am. I have never seen them before this trip, but they seem to be everywhere I go. I also saw Eddie Davis, the guy that works for Mike O'Ryan. He showed up at Irish Kevin's, which is a Key West bar, with the other two men. I'm certain now Mike and Eddie are responsible for those missing tenants. My daughter and I are getting close to Tampa, and we haven't seen them since last night in the bar."

"Celia, without putting yourself or your daughter at risk, try and get a picture of them or their car with their license plate. That will help me in identifying them. You may want to call the State Police and put them on notice, giving them as much detail about these men as you can."

"John, I am no good with descriptions. I have been so frightened I can't even remember what color their car was, plus it was dark outside when I last saw it. I'm also afraid the police won't believe me."

"Celia, I'm going to send you a text with my information. If you can get a photo, send it to my email or text and also send it to Miranda. We'll go from there. Ok?" John continued, "Celia, I don't know if Miranda told you she brought me in to take a look around the apartment building. I have a retired buddy that I called and asked him to stay in an apartment in your building. He has been talking with everyone, flashing money, looking for women- anything to get noticed. He's been in there since you left. He was supposed to update me yesterday, but I was out all day on assignment and wasn't able to touch base. I'm going to call him now and will get back to both of you when I learn anything. In the meantime, Celia your priorities are to be safe, get photos and tag numbers if you can." With that, all three hung up their phones.

CHAPTER 41

When they got back to Kim's apartment in Tampa, Celia helped her daughter put some additional things in her suitcase, along with her books and laptop. Kim called a girlfriend who lived on campus and was relieved when she said Kim could stay with her for a few days.

After they loaded up Kim's car, Celia got in her own car and followed Kim out of the complex. Kim headed toward the college and Celia headed toward the interstate that would take her north.

Celia was exhausted, but she knew she had to get some distance between her and those men if she could.

Picking up I-95 North as she crossed over the Georgia state line, she began looking for exits that showed multiple hotels. Near Brunswick, she saw exit 36A advertising a La Quinta, Days Inn, Motel 6 and a Super 8. As she got off the exit, the first two were fairly close to each other. She would park her car in one lot and pay cash for a room in the other hotel, trying to get a view of the parking lot from her room.

All she needed was a few hours' sleep.

Keslie Patch-Bohrod

CHAPTER 42

After disconnecting the call between Celia, Miranda and himself, John rang up his old friend Claude Fontaine.

Years ago, when John was a secret service agent in the Obama Administration, he had befriended a cyber-expert while working on the case of a crazed domestic terrorist who had tried to bomb the White House. It was Claude's information that led them to the bomber. The incident had occurred many years ago, but they remained in touch. Claude and his wife Hailey purchased a home near John and his wife Lori in Northern New Jersey. Once a month, the four of them got together to play Euchre and have dinner.

When John contacted Claude last week, John had described the disappearances and Claude agreed to stay in an apartment in the Craig's Somerville building and try to uncover evidence relating to the missing tenants. John had also suggested that he check out the Social Security office in Somerville to see if there were any apartment flyers on the bulletin board or if any of the personnel in the office recommended any apartment complexes or services. All three tenants had received Social Security and their checks were direct deposited for their monthly rental payments.

After retiring from the tech company, Claude became a private investigator of sorts. He knew if he didn't keep busy, he would go crazy or die. Sitting around watching television, golfing or fishing wouldn't cut it. He had to have some danger and excitement in his life, although some of his friends said he achieved that goal married to Hailey. She could really be a ball of fire.

While cyber expert might not be considered a dangerous occupation, the focus was secure data, protect the company's networks, watch and stop breaches in the network, and then repair the damage. Now he used his expertise to track and expose hackers and scammers with some of his methods in that grey legal area. He walked a fine line but felt it was worth it in the long run if he had to bend the law to help victims of cybercrimes.

After Miranda handed Claude the keys to the apartment, he returned to his car in the parking lot and opened his trunk. He pulled out his Milwaukee two-wheel folding hand truck and loaded the three large specially designed cases onto the steel toe plate. Over each shoulder, he hung two heavy satchels, and then proceeded to wheel his goods into the apartment building and his new apartment. An hour later, his computers, monitors and routers were set up and operational.

Claude was highly skilled and well versed in the hacking underworld. He had gone after domestic and international groups, identifying locations of operations and bank accounts, surreptitiously handing over the information to law enforcement, FBI and Secret Service. He was known as the Robin Hood of the computer world.

In order to identify the scammers, he would need to gain access to tenants' computers and monitor their activity or somehow get the scammers to interact with him. He thought his first step should be getting known throughout the complex, hanging by the mailboxes at times of delivery, doing laundry in the basement facility and calling maintenance for fictitious repairs. Visiting the local Social Security office was also on his to-do list.

As step one of his plan, he knocked on each neighbor's door around dinner time, asking if anyone saw his cat. He didn't have one, but it gave him an opportunity to introduce himself as a relative of Karen Sinclair and say he was watching her apartment until she could be found. With the doors open he could also sneak a peek inside the apartments, looking for computers. Whoever was making these calls likely had a sophisticated setup.

John had suggested he quickly introduce himself to Mike O'Ryan, not knowing if he was involved. His presence might trigger a response or reaction that might prompt further investigation.

Just two days in, Claude ran into Mike coming from the main office with a large box in his hands.

"Hey, you need a hand with that?" asked Claude.

Startled, Mike quickly responded, "No, all good. Who are you? Are you visiting someone here?"

"No," responded Claude, "I moved into my cousin's apartment to help her out."

"Oh, who's your cousin?" Mike began to get worried. He didn't like unknowns lurking around.

"Karen Sinclair." After Claude mentioned her name, he thought he saw a flicker of recognition or was that fear? "I'm retired too and thought Karen and I could finally learn how to use computers but looks like something might have happened to her. I've been calling all the hospitals in the area, but she hasn't been admitted. Maybe she met some guy and forgot I was coming to visit for a while. I've got nothing but time, and the money to waste it, waiting for her." Claude laughed so that he would appear he wasn't that worried about Karen's disappearance.

"What's your name? "Inquired Mike.

"Claude Fontaine."

"Nice to meet you, I'm Mike O'Ryan and I work here assisting with the rentals. Let me know if you need anything." And with that, Mike left with his box.

Mike immediately got on the phone with Eddie relaying the information about Claude Fontaine, asking him to run his background, cell phone information and see if the guys in the boiler room could get into his computer. Maybe make a phone call saying they were from Comcast, which was Karen's internet provider. Eddie, still chasing Celia with the two investigators, said he would get right on it.

Claude began to make headway on identifying the potential scammers. Tenants he ran into doing laundry told him about receiving PayPal invoices for things they hadn't ordered or other emails from what looked like Microsoft Tech Support informing them they had malware on their computer. Tenants were instructed to call a certain number or click the link to chat with an employee who could resolve the problem.

To Claude, those frauds were commonplace with the perpetrators usually located in India or other foreign countries. Phone links were rerouted all over the world, making it difficult but not impossible to track them down. He had only encountered a few groups operating out of the United States and wondered if this might be true in this case. The only way he could determine the location would be to engage the scammers on the phone or by computer. He asked the tenants to let him know immediately if they received a call or email so he could take a look.

Experience taught him that victims were usually targeted by age with those over fifty tending to be less tech savvy and vulnerable to a number of scams. John had given him the address for the local Social Security office and told him the missing people had recently signed up for their benefits. Claude found several fliers outside the office advertising several apartment buildings, the Craig's being one of them, but with one central phone number. Pulling his cell from his pocket, Claude called and was connected to Mike O'Ryan's voice mail. He left a message using a fake name, disguising his voice, saying he was interested in one of the properties. His scam-o-meter was ticking violently. There was no proof yet, but too many components of this mystery were leading to one place. Now, he could get to work.

CHAPTER 43

Abbeville, South Carolina

Celia got up the next morning, took a quick shower and repacked her things. She was lucky when checking in; the hotel clerk was able to put her in a room that overlooked the parking lot of the Days Inn. She went to the window to check on her car and was horrified to see the two men walking around her car. She went to her purse and pulled out her cell phone and took pictures of them, although from a distance. Then one of the men went to what she assumed was their car, pulled out a brief case and walked to the entrance of The Days Inn. She took pictures of the car and tried to zoom in on the license plate.

Grabbing her bags, she ran down the steps and toward her car, trying to hide behind the other vehicles in the lot. Assuming the men were still inside, probably trying to find out her room number, she quickly put her bags on the back seat, opened her suitcase and pulled out a pair of socks. She crouch-walked over to the back of the men's car and shoved the socks into the tailpipe, hoping this would slow them down. Then, realizing the previous picture from inside the hotel may not be clear enough, she took a better shot of the car and plate then drove away.

Before getting back on the interstate, Celia checked that the men were not following her, pulled off to the side of the road and sent a text to Miranda and John with the photos.

John received the photos while he was in his office and immediately picked up the phone to have one of his colleagues run the plates and try to identify the men. Then he called Miranda.

"Miranda, it's John. I just sent off the pictures of the car and plates to be identified and I can get Georgia and South Carolina State Police after them. In the meantime, we need to find a safe place for Celia until we can catch up with these guys."

"I agree," said Miranda. "I have been thinking the same thing. I have already spoken to my cousin Matt about this, and he thinks it would be a good idea if she came here. John, his place is like a fortress and is very secluded."

"It has to be better than her continuing to drive or staying at a hotel while waiting for the police to get involved. If these guys see that she goes to a police station, they will just disappear or go after her daughter to keep her quiet. Give me the address and phone number there and I will alert the local police department. Let me know when she gets there."

Miranda agreed and called Celia with the address and general directions.

After driving most of the day, Celia finally located the address Miranda had given her. Her GPS said she had arrived but all she saw was a dirt road, gate and lots of trees. As she pulled off the main street toward what she assumed to be the entrance to the property, she heard a voice from the box beside the gate, "Are you Celia?" the voice asked.

"Yes, this is Celia. Is Miranda there?"

"Please pull ahead and take the road to the right up to the house. Miranda will meet you."

As she drove up the long driveway, she was in awe of the dozens of crape myrtle trees lining the roadway. The road forked and she took the one to the right as instructed. She spotted the large house and Miranda standing beside the driveway. Finally, Celia felt grateful to be somewhere safe.

When she got out of the car, she said to Miranda, "I am almost certain I wasn't followed. I drove around Abbeville for an hour, parked, got out of my car and had a cup of coffee at a local café, drove around some more then came here. I haven't seen any cars, frankly."

Miranda took Celia inside the house and introduced her to her cousin and the rest of the family, giving her a brief tour of the kitchen, living room, bathroom, then upstairs to the bedroom where she would sleep that night. They returned to the kitchen as Matt's wife, Allison was putting out food and drinks for everyone. They sat at the dining room table and Miranda asked Celia to start at the beginning and tell what she suspected and what had actually happened.

After her story was complete, Miranda's cousin shook his head and said, "They know exactly where she is; they are not stupid people. These are desperate men who have paid someone well to know what Celia is doing. I would bet my whole estate there is a tracking device on her car and they are waiting for dark to ambush us. We only have a few hours of daylight to make a plan and wait for them. The first order is a tour of my property, and I will conduct a perimeter check as we go. "

They left the house and got in a golf cart by the garage. As they were driving, Matt said, "The previous owner fenced the entire estate and had cameras installed at strategic points. The front gate is controlled at the main house, which is how I let you in. I could see who you were when you drove up. I want to warn you not to venture out too far from the house on your own, there are wild pigs on the property, and I have been trapping three to four every night. They are feral, with tusks, and are extremely dangerous. There is a huge population of big Tuskers in South Carolina, and I swear most of them have made their home on my land. These bad boys are ravenous and tear apart my back fields every night. They have tried to get at our livestock and trash, so we have everything locked up tight. Boars are an aggressive species, and they carry all sorts of diseases like tuberculosis, hepatitis E and influenza A. The two hundred fifty pound adult males will have huge tusks and can run as fast as twenty-five miles an hour. We generally only see them when they come out at night in search of food- which might be small reptiles, rodents and mammals. We have to be especially careful with our ducks and fowl in the barn because they also like to eat eggs. And since this is the beginning of their rutting season, there is a greater chance they will attack. "

"Can't you poison them somehow?" asked Miranda.

"Because they are such a nuisance, people have been trying everything to get rid of them. There are all sorts of new baits and traps that can be remotely activated. Research into pesticides was done in Australia because they have so many. They studied the use of sodium nitrite and Warfarin, which also has been tested here in the United States. Problem is some pesticides are really cruel in how they kill, and others pose a danger to other animals. So, none of them have been approved for use in any state. Warfarin, which is used as a blood thinner in humans, and is also used as a poison for rats, takes days and large quantities to kill the boar. Sodium nitrite in the required quantity basically suffocates the animal. The problem with either of these is how to deliver it to the hogs while avoiding the other animals, birds and plants in the area. So, I just use my old traps and a bullet to the brain. Oh, and by the way, we also have snapping turtles in the pond so don't go wading or dangling your feet in the water from the dock or center island."

Miranda always suspected her cousin was some sort of a survivalist and that was why he chose this property. The house sat high on a hill overlooking the back of the estate, giving it the perfect vantage point if someone were to approach from any angle or direction.

When Miranda took the grand tour earlier, she also had a chance to view the barns, the livestock, and woods. She saw the gun safe, knives and butchering equipment that her cousin had stockpiled. The wild pigs that were caught had been killed, dressed and eaten. Waste not, want not. The freezer was also stocked with venison, rabbit and quail. This property was a real hunter's paradise. Miranda was certain that her cousin was an expert shot, as were his wife and kids. You don't live on a property like this and not be able to handle a gun and a knife.

They returned to the house and before they moved inside, Matt said, "Celia hand me your keys. I want to check your car then move it into the garage where it will be out of sight." Celia gave him the keys and watched as he opened the car, inspecting the inside. He looked under the hood, then got on the ground and slid under the car. After a few minutes, he slid out again holding what looked like some type of electronic device.

"Yeah, I thought they would be tracking you. I am going to take this inside and try to dismantle it; I don't want to destroy it because someone might be able to find out who these guys are by looking at this thing. There may be a serial number that might lead to the manufacturer, distributor and then finally to the purchaser."

"They must have found out where Kim lived in Tampa and put it on my car. I guess that's why they were constantly looking for us in Key West. We drove Kim's car there and parked it behind the hotel. They wouldn't have known where we were staying if they

160

couldn't track my car. Once I picked up my car in Tampa, they saw I was on the move and would be able to track my movements. You don't think Kim is in danger, do you?" asked Celia.

"Celia, anything is possible. But my guess is that they are around here now. Why don't you call her and see if she is alright? You said she was staying on campus with a friend. They probably have no idea where she is. I will call John and let him know that Matt found a tracking device on your car and ask him to notify the Tampa police to keep an eye on Kim. Give me her friend's phone number and I will pass that along. Why don't you go in the bedroom and give her a call?" suggested Miranda.

When Celia left the room, Miranda and Matt shared knowing looks. He walked over to the gun safe and removed several rifles, shot guns and a cross bow. He handed out walkie-talkies to each person and instructed the group to set up on the wrap around porch outside of the living room and watch a specific part of the property. If they saw any movement whatsoever, they were to notify him immediately.

Miranda got John Franklin on the phone and told him Celia had made it safely to her cousin's place. She had already given him the address so he could notify the authorities in the Abbeville area. She next told him of their concerns for Kim's safety. These men might go after her to lure Celia.

"Miranda, if these guys are so smart, why didn't they find Kim's car information or hotel reservation?" asked John.

Celia had returned to the great room and overheard John's question. Miranda had the conversation on speaker phone.

"I was wondering the same thing," admitted Celia. "Maybe it's because she has my husband's last name, so they might not have known that. I took back my maiden name after the divorce and I haven't mentioned Kim's last name to anyone including Greg Baker or Miranda. The car and the credit cards she used for the hotel reservation are in her name."

"I was able to run a check on that car," reported John. "It was stolen in New Jersey so that won't help identify these men until we can catch them. I have given the plate, car make and model to the

161

state police who will be coming to Matt's house as soon as they can get there."

"John, this whole thing started when Celia began looking into the records in the various apartment buildings. The only people who knew she was researching the leasing information were Greg Baker and Mike O'Ryan of O'Ryan Realty Placement Services. There might be a connection with either of these men. Maybe you can find out if there have been any complaints against them and what the result was. And could you also do me huge favor? Let Jack know what is going on and that I will call later. We are kind of busy here right now trying to avoid an ambush."

"I will pass on the information to Jack. I spoke with my friend Claude this morning. He has been busy digging and is convinced Mike O'Ryan is doing something with the victim's Social Security checks and running other scams. If anyone can find out what is going on, he can," assured John.

Miranda hung up the phone, picked up her walkie-talkie and grabbed a rifle. Looking it over, she saw that it was a Savage 110 Lightweight Storm. It had been many years since she had fired a weapon, but she knew she could if she had to. It didn't have any aiming sights, but she guessed at the distance she would be shooting, sights wouldn't matter. Matt must have bought this gun for Allison based on its weight, short barrel and that it would work for a variety of game. Living out in this wilderness, the entire family had to be prepared for whatever might pop up in their backyard.

CHAPTER 44

Phil and Jerry had not been able to locate the hotel where Celia and her daughter were staying in Key West. They hadn't been given much information to go on, just the make, model, color of her car, Celia's general physical description and that she would be traveling with a college age young woman.

Their instructions were clear. Find her, get rid of her. Get rid of the body and the car. If need be, get rid of the daughter as well.

She hadn't used her credit card anywhere in Key West, so they began their search by approaching the front desks of the better known hotels asking for two women who met their description. They provided different reasons for their interest; we hit their car, there was a family emergency, but with privacy policies as they were now, they had no luck. They also couldn't locate the car the women were driving; they must have taken the daughter's car. There was no record of a Kim Ravenscroft with the Department of Motor Vehicles so either she didn't have a driver's license, or she had a different last name.

Key West had been crowded and not the most conducive for a quick, clean kill. Eddie had insisted that they check out of their hotel, get some bags of food and water and stake out a place on Route 1 North where they could watch for the women. If they left town at night, it would be difficult to see the faces of the people in cars as they passed by but maybe they could tell if it was two women.

Each man took a two-hour shift. It had been a long, slow night with sparse traffic on the highway. Finally, about eight thirty that morning, they spotted Celia and her daughter driving by. Careful not to be seen, Phil, who was in the driver's seat, allowed four cars to pass before pulling onto the road. Traffic being brutal on Route 1, more and more cars entered the roadway behind Celia, making it extremely difficult to keep an eye on her vehicle. Cars were basically bumper to bumper going twenty-five miles an hour, in a stop and go pattern.

As Celia's car seemed to slip away from them, Eddie grew more and more agitated. Phil kept reminding him, they installed a tracker on her car back in Tampa so she wouldn't be able to totally slip away. Not giving him solace, the assurances at least kept him from continuing to berate the two investigators.

The thugs finally caught up with her in Georgia but hadn't counted on the bitch stuffing socks in the exhaust pipe of their car. They were almost certain she was still in the Days Inn. Eddie had gone to the breakfast area of the motel to pick up some coffee and sandwiches and Phil and Lester had gone to the front desk to find out what room she was in.

As Eddie was paying for the food and drinks, Mike called him on his cell phone. "I take it you haven't finished the job yet?"

"No, but we are close. She's in this motel in Georgia. Phil and Lester are getting her room number right now," reported Eddie.

"I have had enough of these two incompetents. You need to find a quiet place, get rid of them and then take care of Celia yourself. This is dragging on way too long."

Just then, Eddie heard Phil yell out, "Hey, she's leaving! She was at the other hotel!"

"Mike, got to go, she's on the run. I think we have her now," yelled Eddie as he disconnected the call.

They ran out, jumped in their car, and inserted the key. Nothing. Lester was fairly good with cars, so he got out of the car and popped the hood to take a look. He figured she had taken the distributor cap, but it was still there. He checked all the connections, checked the gas tank and gauge but he couldn't figure out why the car wouldn't start.

With no other option, he crawled under the car and examined every inch of the under carriage until he came to the back. That's when he spotted the clogged tailpipe. Boy that was an old trick. He hadn't heard of that being done for years. He'd have to remember that. As he was removing the socks, Eddie shouted to him from the back seat, "While you are at it, steal a couple more license plates and change these out. We can't be too careful; she could have written down the plate information."

Over an hour had been wasted and they had to make up time by speeding through Georgia into South Carolina. This chase had gone on long enough. They needed to catch up to her soon and finish this job.

Celia had made a few stops at various rest stops and a café for a cup of coffee. Things were looking up because it appeared she was headed into the boondocks where it would be perfect for her to disappear without a trace. Eddie was thinking the same thing about getting rid of Phil and Lester. It all had to be done soon before she had a chance to get back to New Jersey or pass along any information she might have. They didn't think she would jeopardize her daughter's life by telling her what she suspected. If she did, they could also go back and kill the kid.

The men had no idea where she was going, if she was meeting someone or just trying to give them the slip. The GPS coordinates from the tracking device pointed them to a dirt road in Abbeville and indicated she was somewhere in a forested area. There was a closed gate along the road and fencing but nothing else to tell them what lay beyond.

Phil parked their car down the road along an area with some overgrowth, making it difficult for their vehicle to be spotted from the gate or from the main road. Eddie figured there was no time like the present. Phil and Lester were seated in the front seats and Eddie was directly behind Phil, who was still in the driver's seat. Both men had to be distracted so that Eddie could kill them both without getting himself injured or killed in the process. Each of them had their weapons drawn, ready to get out of the car.

Taking a deep breath, Eddie said, "I think the two of you should first check out that side road over there on the left." As the men looked to the left, Eddie raised his pistol, and shot Lester in the head. When Phil reacted to the sound and turned his head to the right to see what happened, Eddie shot him in the temple.

With that job done, it was clean up time. First the dead men's guns were removed from their hands, careful not to smudge the prints; it might be helpful at a later time to use the guns to implicate them in Celia's death. Eddie got out of the car and went to the trunk to remove the equipment and weapons. There were a few rags inside which he used to try and clean up the blood from the windshield. No use alerting a passerby that something happened here. Finally, he dragged the men one at a time from the car and stuffed them into the trunk.

At a distance, Eddie inspected the gate and surrounding area, spotting what looked like a closed-circuit television camera camouflaged by some greenery. Not sure if his image was being picked up, he thought his best bet would be to follow the fence and see if there were any openings, or a place where he could cut the fence and enter the property. In the bag taken from the trunk of the car were night vision goggles, wire cutters, guns and ammunition. Eddie slung one of the rifles over his shoulder and began to walk the perimeter of the property. When he came upon a camera along the fence line, he used the butt of the rifle to smash it. After about twenty minutes of walking, a spot was found in the fence where he could crawl through with his bag of weapons. All he had to do now was to hunker down and wait until it got dark.

CHAPTER 45

Everyone took a place on the floor of the balcony overlooking the back of the property. Matt instructed them on how to use the walkie-talkies and what section of the property they were to watch.

"I have spotlights around the property that will turn on when there is movement. It is my intention to shoot if someone comes on my land without my permission. I will protect my family and friends who are here. You all need to be incredibly careful with your weapons and know who you are pointing them at. I am going out over to the left, crossing over the pasture and I will begin to patrol the woods to the back, eventually moving forward to the house. I know where the motion sensors are and will be able to avoid them. If they go on, you will know it is not me. Now that it is approaching dark, we will shut off all the lights in the house. That is to prevent you from being silhouetted and a potential target. Please try not to make any noise and be very patient." Matt left the group to begin his reconnaissance.

The sun had set at five forty-one. Inside the perimeter of the fence, surrounded by trees and brush, it was totally black. Eddie donned his night vision goggles and began moving slowly through the wooded area. His plan was to scout the property for any buildings or a house. From the trek along the fence line, he knew it was a large area and it might take him all night to find what and who he was looking for. The GPS tracking device on the car had gone dead for some reason, so Eddie had to proceed blind.

Two hours later, working in a grid pattern, he eyed an opening in the trees ahead. Eddie moved to the left of the tree line. There seemed to be a dark silhouette just in front of him. As he approached farther toward the clearing a series of motion detection lights came on, blinding him. Eddie had to rip the NVGs off his head and fall to the ground, waiting for his vision to clear. Faint noises could be heard, but he couldn't tell the direction.

Eddie decided to keep moving forward on the side of the tree line toward the large, dark shape, guessing it was a building of some type, hopefully, where Celia was staying. This place was really giving him the creeps. With all the cameras and motion detection lights this might be some kind of secure facility he thought. For what, he didn't know; he just wanted to get the lady and get out of there.

Matt figured out whoever was out there would search from the back of the property and work forward until they found the house. He turned off his walkie-talkie, this way his location wouldn't be given away if someone from the house tried to contact him. When he saw the motion lights come on, his guess was confirmed. He moved along the right side of the property quickly as he searched. Matt silently chuckled to himself thinking of all the possible outcomes to what he considered an adventure. This back wood was no playground for the uninitiated. Whoever was out there didn't know what they were in for.

As Matt continued along, he began to hear some rustling of the undergrowth ahead. The noise was too loud to be human; it had to be the pigs. Matt chuckled again as he moved closer. He would herd the pigs toward the house and whoever was up ahead. This was going to be fun, he thought to himself. He hoped Miranda wouldn't get too angry with him.

Matt had loaded his pockets with feed pellets earlier and as he got within sight of the wild pigs, he noticed a man crouched near a tree by the clearing. He began to toss a few pellets in the direction where the man was hiding.

The pigs scurried to the pellets, and he could hear them snuffling as they ate. He threw more and waited. The man was just up ahead moving toward the house. He threw another handful that landed near the man's feet. Matt knew these pigs would prefer bigger game to pellets and sat down on the ground and watched.

Eddie was intent on making his way toward the building and was not paying attention to the little noises of the woods. When small objects began dropping by his feet, he knew something strange was happening. Eddie spotted the pigs and at the same time spotted the large metal wire boxes in the clearing. His first thought was that those pigs looked mean. His second thought was that he better take cover in one of those cages over there. Maybe they were like shark cages and prevented the pigs from reaching anyone inside. He lifted the side of the trap and crawled underneath. Letting the trap fall to the ground, he felt confident the pigs couldn't fit their snouts through the wire and bite him. What he didn't know, was that each trap had a baited entrance behind him, worked like a roach motel, allowing the pigs to enter but not leave.

Eddie became a big man confined in the small, round cage. When the pigs approached, he couldn't maneuver his guns in the tight space to fire outward at the pigs.

Hungry, feral pigs had one goal; to make Eddie their Monday night dinner. Finding the special opening into the trap, they entered and began sampling New Jersey's finest vermin.

Matt sat there and listened to the sound of the man screaming while the pigs feasted on Eddie's flesh. After a few minutes, he rose, pulled a pistol from the waist band of his pants and walked over to the boar trap. He carefully shot each wild pig in the head and walked back to the house, shouting, "It's me, Matt, don't shoot!"

Miranda looked at the expression on Matt's face as he came into the house and said somewhat scolding, "Matt, what did you do?"

"Miranda, I couldn't believe it. That darn fool crawled into the boar trap. By the time I got there, those pigs were in a feeding frenzy. We better call an ambulance and the police. He still might be alive to answer some questions."

When the police and ambulance arrived, Matt met them at the gate in his golf cart and escorted them through the back field to the boar trap.

The pigs were dead and covered not only with their blood from Matt's shot, but the blood of the man they had been gorging on.

Matt explained that the man had been tracking Celia and was probably a contract killer. Once Matt knew that someone had entered his property, he tried to intercept him but the pigs got to him first. As soon as Matt saw the man was in the trap, he killed the wild boars.

Miranda called Jack to let him know she was all right, and then called John for his assistance in dealing with the local police. John had been in contact with them shortly before Matt called for help, so there was no need for her to worry.

After the intruder was stabilized, loaded in the ambulance and rushed to the nearest hospital, the police began to take statements from everyone staying at Matt's house. Around three in the morning, a call came in that two men were found in the trunk of an abandoned car about a mile from the entrance to Matt's property. The sheriff returned to the house.

"There's only one way to figure out who these guys are, so Ms. Ravenscroft, if you wouldn't mind coming with me, I will have you take a look and see if you can identify them."

Celia agreed. Miranda accompanied her in the sheriff's car. The bodies had already been bagged and were being loaded into a coroner's van when they arrived at the scene. The sheriff motioned for the men to unzip the bags for Celia to take a look.

She let out a gasp and said, "Those are the two men that were following me! So, if they are here and dead, who is the other one? Could it be Eddie Davis, I did see him with them in the Keys?"

"Not quite sure we know," responded the sheriff. "The one in the trap is pretty badly mutilated from those pigs and he had no identification on him. We will have to wait until he gets to the hospital, so he can be treated and printed, that is, if he survives."

While climbing up the stairs to the main house, now that the ordeal was over, Miranda turned to Matt and said, "Good time?"

Matt chuckled and said, "Cuz, I haven't had that much fun since I don't know when!"

After a good night sleep, Miranda insisted on driving back to New Jersey with Celia. This would give her time to help Celia decompress from the last few weeks, and hopefully come up with a plan.

CHAPTER 46

From his experience, Claude knew boiler rooms operated twenty-four seven, with crews rotating in and out every eight hours. He was certain that with the number of complaints the tenants had reported to him, someone would contact him soon.

He had almost finished preparing dinner, with a whiskey and soda, when his phone rang. It was Cindy, Allister Foley's neighbor.

"Claude, Bill just got a popup on his computer saying his version of Windows software is damaged and obsolete. All system files will be automatically deleted in three hundred and ten seconds."

"Thanks, Cindy. I'll be right down. Tell Bill not to touch anything. Does he have a camera on his PC or laptop?" asked Claude.

"Yes, he does."

"Please tell him to make sure whoever may be watching can't see me entering your apartment. I will be down in a minute." Claude hurriedly disconnected his laptop and grabbed his phone. As he entered Cindy and Bill's apartment, he accessed their Wi-Fi then called John Franklin to tell him he had a fish on the hook and to stand by.

Thinking how to approach the situation, Claude whispered, "Somehow cover the camera so we can switch places."

Bill had the computer monitor on a desk under a window. He moved the curtains so they covered the top of the portion of the screen, effectively blocking his image from view by the camera.

Claude took his place at the desk. On the screen, he saw instructions to click the update button to install the newest software. This software would then scan and protect files from being deleted. He clicked the button and a new popup window appeared announcing he had three viruses on his machine and needed to call tech support at 800-555-2743 to pay for the complete version of the new software that would fix the problem.

Calling the number, Claude was connected with Ramon, who informed him "I need to check your computer to see if it is still under warranty. You will need to fill out this form providing me with your name, address and credit card information. While you are doing that, I can make a secure connection to run system diagnostics."

"Oh, OK. Anything, I just need my computer fixed, "Claude responded. He turned and looked at Cindy and Bill with a big smile.

Claude used a process to reverse engineer the connection after Ramon gained remote access to the computer, thus allowing Claude to see everything Ramon was doing. He was also able to record voice and keystrokes, while he rummaged around in all of Ramon's files. This was the part that Claude loved the most, finding the IP address, physical location and Ramon's internet provider. He was even able to find an image in one of the files of a cable company document showing name, addresses, mobile phone number, where and when the installs took place and customer number. Pay dirt! And the bonus, they were local addresses.

As Ramon continued to talk about damaged files and how much the software fix would cost, Claude placed a call to John Franklin, telling him where to find the scammers. Claude would keep Ramon engaged until the police arrived. He would ask all sorts of silly questions that would require long explanations.

Ramon thought Claude had no clue what was happening, but in actuality he could see each file opened and what bank accounts were being accessed. Just as Ramon asked Claude to enter his credit card information, he heard a ruckus in the background. A few minutes passed and John Franklin called Claude's cell phone.

"I called Detective Morris right away. He had a warrant already to present to a judge; he just had to fill in the blanks with location, business and the other miscellaneous information. Claude, I think I'm going to need you down here to help sort this out. We have eight guys working phones and computers. I'm fairly sure this is a bogus company. You will be able to tell us more." John let out a deep breath. "Let's hope this implicates who we think is behind this."

CHAPTER 47

Celia was finally able to retrieve the phone message from Greg as she and Miranda were driving into New Jersey. She tried to reach him on his cell but there was no answer. This was strange because the way he worded his message she was certain he would answer no matter what. She was familiar with the bank he did business with, so she called to see if possibly he was in a meeting and had shut his phone off for some reason. The bank representative informed her of the incident and that he had been rushed to the hospital. There was no word as to his condition.

Celia was in panic mode. "Miranda, I wonder if Greg getting sick has anything to do with the missing tenants. He told me he wanted to talk about the reports Mike gave him. I know from my brief review of Greg's records that something looked fishy. I originally wondered if both Mike and Greg were up to something but now, I know it's just Mike."

"Celia, we are almost to Somerville. Why don't we stop in the office, see if we can find some of the records Greg was talking about. I'm also worried about your safety here. Whoever is after you will be watching your apartment, the hospital and me. I think you need to hide out somewhere. I'll call John again."

Once they picked up Mike's report from Greg's office, some other documents he had included with them, and the records regarding the Craig's apartment building, Celia decided to pick up a few things from her place.

Celia went directly into the kitchen, opened her refrigerator and took out a bottle of water, offering one to Miranda. "No thanks, I'm fine. I just want to get you out of here. I don't think you are safe. After glancing at those records and what you told me in South Carolina, I think this O'Ryan guy is transferring these tenants' Social Security payments to his own account somewhere. I also have a sneaking suspicion that he has killed them. The message from Greg also leads me to believe he suspects Mike of something, and that may have somehow led to his hospitalization. The sooner I get you somewhere remote, the better you will be until John can get a handle on this. I'm going to call him right now and see where I should take you."

Celia took her water into the bathroom where she took a long drink and began to load a cosmetics bag with her toothbrush, toothpaste and few other essential items. She finished the water and threw the bottle in the recycling bin.

As she passed by, Miranda said, "John suggests I take you to my house in Warren. He'll meet us there as soon as he can. He also told me Claude's findings so far are consistent with what we suspect. They found a boiler room where a number of men have been making the calls our tenants were complaining about. He has Claude going through all the computer files hoping to find names of the people in charge. There seems to be a number of fraudulent scams coming out of this group. He's working on gathering evidence on where the money is and agrees that it includes some kind of Social Security fraud."

Celia went back into the kitchen and grabbed another bottle and opened it. "I am so thirsty; I guess I didn't hydrate enough on our drive north. I can't seem to quench my thirst." She drank some more water on her way into the bedroom. She put the bottle on the nightstand and began to pull out some underwear and socks. As she was walking into the closet, she had to grab ahold of the door to steady herself.

"Miranda, I feel so lightheaded and nauseous," said a woozy Celia.

"I think you have had a traumatic two weeks and you need some time to decompress. Let's get your bag and get out of here. Do you want me to get you some more water?" asked Miranda. With an affirmative response, she took two more bottles out of the refrigerator and handed them to Celia.

Celia continued to drink the water as they drove to Warren. Miranda called Jack and told him what she had planned, and that John was coming to the house. Jack promised to join them after he finished with a client.

It was early evening when they arrived, and Miranda was anxious to prepare dinner and get some sleep. As she opened the pantry door, Miranda heard a loud bang. Celia fell to the floor and began to seize uncontrollably. Miranda rushed to her, feeling for a pulse which seemed quite slow to her. She ran to the living room and pulled her phone out of her purse and dialed 911 for paramedics. Thankfully, the local EMS squad came quickly; their station was only a mile and a half away. They rushed Celia to Overlook Hospital in Summit. Miranda called Jack while she drove behind the emergency vehicle. He would get in touch with John and meet them there.

In the Emergency Room, doctors began to work on Celia. The EMT's had already set up an intravenous line in the rig. The physicians drew blood and threaded a catheter to collect urine for testing.

Miranda had had the foresight to grab the water bottles Celia had been drinking, thinking it was the only thing Celia had that she hadn't. Could she have been poisoned? She also called John one more time; hoping he wasn't annoyed with her constant phone calls. She suggested he send someone to Celia's apartment to search for anything that might be the cause of Celia's seizure. She also told him that Celia's boss, Greg Baker, had been rushed to the hospital in Somerville after collapsing at a local bank and that he should determine if there were any similarities between the two events. Had he been drinking bottled water from the apartment, as well?

Miranda approached one of the nurses at the Emergency Room desk and handed her the water bottles. "Would you please give these to the physicians that are taking care of Celia Ravenscroft. You probably want to have them check to see if there is anything in the water that could have caused the symptoms she is experiencing. It is the only food and drink she had in the past six hours." The nurse nodded, grabbed the bottles and ran off to the operatory where Celia was being treated.

Keslie Patch-Bohrod

CHAPTER 48

John Franklin called Claude and asked him to meet him at Celia Ravenscroft's apartment. Waiting for the police to search Celia's apartment was not an option at this point. Her life might be hanging by a thread if they couldn't determine what caused her and possibly Greg's collapse. He had called Detective Morris to inform him that Miranda had given him permission to enter the apartment since it was technically part of the leasing office. Anything found would be handled properly and submitted for evidence.

Donning latex gloves, John and Claude entered Celia and Greg's apartment. At first glance nothing seemed amiss. They began to systematically search each room from top to bottom, taking special notice in the kitchen and bathroom. Miranda had informed John that she thought something might be in the water Celia had been drinking, since that was the only thing Miranda had not consumed that Celia had.

John noticed a bottle of eye drops on the kitchen counter. He strode into the bathroom to see if there were additional bottles there. Finding two more in the trash can, he carefully put them into an evidence bag for a technician to check for prints and to confirm the contents of the bottles. Nothing else was found that might lead to a medical emergency. Celia had no medications, no dangerous cleaning products or bug sprays; she didn't even have a bottle of bleach.

Claude came out of the bedroom and said, "Hey John, I noticed that there are men's clothes in the closet and men's toiletries in the bathroom. Do you know if she had a boyfriend or husband?"

"Yes, she is living with Greg Baker. He owns a number of apartment complexes in the area. Mysteriously, he too has taken ill and is in intensive care at Robert Wood Johnson. Let's drop this stuff off at the station so it can get tagged and analyzed, and then go to the hospital. We should see if we can find out anything about his condition. Let's swing by the bank where he went down and check if any of his belongings were left there, especially food or drink items."

An hour later, the attending physician, Dr. Burrows, came out of Celia's hospital room looking tired but with a slight smile on his face.

He spoke with Miranda and Jack who had been sitting patiently on the couch in the waiting room. "I really can't give you any information about your friend because of HIPPA regulations, but she is stable at this time, but remains unconscious. We have the water bottles being analyzed in the lab and I hope to have some details in the next hour or two. I have been contacted by the police and will keep them informed best I can. I suggest you go home, there is nothing you can do right now."

"Doctor, Celia has a daughter named Kim. I don't know her last name, but I am going to try to reach her and tell her about her mother's condition. She will probably get in touch with you soon." Miranda pulled out Celia's cellphone; she had taken it from her purse shortly after she collapsed at their house. She would find Kim's number and phone her while she and Jack drove home.

CHAPTER 49

Sitting at the dining room table eating takeout pizza and drinking a bottle of Napa Cabernet, Jack asked, "So how was the wedding?"

Miranda laughed so hard she almost peed her pants, and then started to cry. "Oh, Jack the wedding was beautiful, and it was wonderful to see my family, but this whole apartment thing is just dreadful. It really put a damper on our family get together at Matt's house. People are missing and probably dead, and Celia and Greg are both in a bad way. What are we going to do? Whoever is doing this may come after us next."

"John is working with the local police" Jack said as he poured more wine. "You have trusty Maynard to keep an eye on you. Just make sure to set the alarm when you get home or when you leave. I'll call our neighbors and ask them to keep their eyes open for anything suspicious."

"We never should have purchased this apartment building. We are never around and I'm not sure I'm up to the task of being a property manager. If Greg survives, let's ask him if he would buy it back." Jack put his arms around Miranda and held her while she sobbed.

"I know it has been a horrible few months, especially for you. I really don't know how you have managed to hold yourself together until now. Let's try and get some sleep and see how the world looks tomorrow. Maybe John will have some news and Celia and Greg will show improvement. It's all we can hope for right now."

Jack gave Miranda a kiss and walked her upstairs to bed. After he tucked her in, he went back downstairs, recycled the pizza box and empty wine bottle. He let Maynard out and watched while he did his business. Jack made sure to check that the outside gate was latched securely and did a spot check around the backyard. He remembered Maynard had been poisoned and hospitalized over the summer, which had led to Miranda at the shore alone and unprotected. She had been attacked and he was not going to let that happen again. Maynard might look like a Chocolate Labrador, but his personality and genetics were more Weimaraner, that of a big game hunting dog. He was fiercely protective of Miranda, and Jack was sure the dog wouldn't let anyone get to Miranda if he could help it. Once inside, Jack set the house security alarm, put on the outside lights and went to bed.

CHAPTER 50

"Eddie, what the hell is going on? I haven't heard from you in days! I was counting on you. And what happened to those two losers I hired to kill Celia while she was on vacation? They had two weeks and so many opportunities, but they couldn't make it happen. Call me!!" Mike hung up the phone after leaving yet another message for Eddie.

Later that day, Mike saw a news report on CNN about two men being found shot to death in the trunk of a car. The report included a story about another man eaten by wild boars in South Carolina. He closed his eyes and shook his head, thinking 'This can't be happening. God help me, what next? A plague of locusts or the Black Death?'

Pigs? Who gets eaten by pigs? Well at least they couldn't be tied to him. Now he just had to figure out what to do next. He logged into his offshore bank accounts. He had a tidy seven million socked away and had another five hundred thousand to add to it. All he had to do was collect the cash, pay Eddie what he owed him, if he was alive and not in police custody. Then slip quickly and quietly out of town. The heat was turning up and there was no way to reach Greg and Celia to finish them off. With all the camera surveillance nowadays and police presence, he couldn't take the chance. If he destroyed Greg and Celia's records as well as his own, the police would have a hard time piecing it all together. The remaining direct deposits in effect were all legitimate, going into Greg's and the Craig's accounts. He hadn't had time to make his move on any of them. The money trail would be hard to follow because he took every precaution. His first order of business had been to set up a number of shell companies registered in different countries. Bank accounts for those companies came next. Money was routinely moved from one location to another then finally to a numbered account in Switzerland. Maybe he could hack into a bank in South Dakota and two other states and set up some bogus accounts using the names and Social Security numbers of the tenants he killed. The police might think those tenants were still alive. He would have to think this out and work fast. First, he had to call his lead guy in the boiler room to have him send everyone home, destroy all the phones, computers and shred the paperwork. None of the workers had any clue who he was. He used public transportation whenever he went to check on their work so they couldn't trace him through his car. He really covered his tracks. He could always set it up again in another state after things quieted down.

CHAPTER 51

Miranda had all the records for their apartment building and Greg's business at her house but hadn't had a chance to review them in detail or let John even know she had them. With Celia still in the hospital she wasn't sure when she would be able to take a look at them. Kim would be arriving soon from Florida to be with her mother. Miranda wanted to be there, not only to show her support, but to get more information as to Celia's condition since the doctors would only tell her next of kin. She would call John from the hospital to inform him about any new details and begin to review the documents while in the visitor's waiting room.

But first, Maynard needed to go to the dog park across town. He had been housebound way too much lately because of the cold weather. He needed the stimulation of the dog park. Hopefully, a few other dogs would be there so he could play and chase them around. She could spare the time.

Grabbing her purse, phone and leash, she loaded Maynard into the car, forgetting to set the security system. The park was only about five minutes from the house, so she figured on letting Maynard wander around for fifteen or twenty minutes, then would drop him back home. Within the hour she would be headed to the hospital. She sent Jack a text letting him know her plans.

Miranda parked the car in the parking lot of the East County Park. Maynard was extremely excited in the back seat; this was his favorite place, other than the dog park in Barnegat Light on Long Beach Island. She imagined all the smells that stimulated him. Not just the people, who walked and ran on the path, but the dogs and other animals that roamed around the park. As she opened the back door, she had to physically block Maynard from darting out of the car. Putting his leash around his neck and the Gentle Leader Headcollar around his snout, she finally let him jump out of the car. She remembered back to the days when she was training him as a puppy to walk on the leash. He would pull so much that he would choke himself. She tried different collar types and harnesses, but nothing stopped him from pulling. While they were walking around a park in Basking Ridge, a friend of hers suggested she try the Gentle Leader her dog was wearing.

They traded collars and at once Maynard was a different dog. It slowed him down, seemed comfortable and he no longer choked himself on the leash.

They began to walk the path toward the dedicated dog area which had two fenced-in sections of land about a five minute walk from the parking lot. The park was deserted. Miranda guessed it was too cold, or people came at different times during the day.

Miranda opened the gate to the first fenced in area and walked Maynard inside. She removed his leash and let him roam. He began his investigative sniffing of the dogs that had been there before him. He quickly started marking his territory, and Miranda grabbed a few poop bags because she knew what would occur next. While she waited for him to do his business, she spotted a jogger on one of the other paths. Relaxing a bit with the company, she realized how creepy it was being alone here. Sure, it was wide open space, but it was all the trees surrounding the park that bothered her. There was an emergency phone station somewhere, but she had never taken the time to find it. She quickly looked around the area. It wasn't by the dog park, so that would not be of help. Just as she was going to take her phone out of her pocket, Maynard squatted. She pulled out the poop bag, cleaned up his mess and walked out of the gated area over to the trash can. The jogger had just reached the dog run and said to her "Wow, what a great looking dog, what kind is it?"

As was habit, she looked over to where Maynard was standing and began to tell the person, "He is a…" when she felt a stab of pain in her neck. Turning to look at the jogger, she only glimpsed a figure in a grey hooded sweatshirt, the face was covered by a scarf. That would be the last thing she remembered.

CHAPTER 52

Mike had been watching Miranda's house from the moment he learned that Celia was in the hospital instead of the morgue. He had to make sure she didn't get ahold of any of the records. It would be a disaster if she found any incriminating documents. He had to be certain and would search her house when the opportunity arose. Last night, Mike broke into Greg's office and removed all the circuit boards from his computer and laptop. He also removed any documents showing his business dealings with Greg. Rummaging through the desk he found a number of memory sticks he was sure Greg used to back up his computers. Then he drove to Celia's place and did the same thing. The longer he could keep the police from linking his actual work to Greg and Celia the better. If there were no records of his dealings with Greg, he could tell the police they were still negotiating a contract. Mike was worried there might be some trace evidence still in the three apartments of the tenants he and Eddie killed. He decided out of an overabundance of caution, to set fire to the apartment building, collectively taking care of everything. It was during the day, so many of the tenants would be out and those inside would surely hear and respond to the smoke and fire alarms.

He returned to the Craig's house at six that morning and saw the husband drive away a few hours later, presumably to work. Now Miranda was leaving, and it looked like she had the dog with her. Keeping a safe distance as he followed her, he saw Miranda pull into the park's main entrance. Maybe his luck would hold out and she would be going to the dog park. He remembered how secluded it was and maybe he could get her out of the way long enough that he could search their house. However, it wouldn't do for her to see him too soon. He would go to the other entrance by the soccer fields, park his car there and pretend to be a jogger. Maybe he would be able to sneak up on her some way.

From his parking lot, Mike could make out that Miranda and the dog were heading to the dog run. He pulled his bag from the passenger seat, unzipped it and took out the syringe he had prepared last night. He always kept a few ampules of Ketamine around for just such an occasion. It was great for knocking someone out quickly without killing them- the classic date rape drug. He didn't have to kill Miranda; he was almost certain she didn't really know how his business was tied into her apartment ownership. Just to make sure, he would search her house as soon as he immobilized her. No evidence, no conviction.

Exiting his car, Mike studied the grounds around him making sure he was alone. This place was as deserted as it had been the last time he was there. He began to jog leisurely toward Miranda. She really wasn't paying too much attention to him. He would have to try to play it cool until he could get close enough to her. He watched the dog squat to poop. She would have to leave the enclosed area to dispose of the bag and that would be the best time to approach her. Mike took a closer look at the dog. It seemed tame enough. It looked like a Chocolate Lab, and they were known to be such pussy dogs- friends to burglars.

As Miranda approached the trash can, Mike jogged a bit faster toward her. He asked her what kind of dog she had, and as she looked away, he stabbed the needle into her neck. Pretty slick, he thought to himself. When she fell, he decided he had better get her body hidden over in the ravine, where no one would see her for a while. Dragging her over the sidewalk onto the grassy area by the tree line, he began to lift her to throw her over a row of bushes when the dog began to bark fervently. That dog would need to be taken care of; it could alert someone to Miranda's body in short order and he would need time to search her house. The woman's body rolled down the hill and as he was turning to address the barking dog, Maynard took a running jump and leaped over the four foot fence at Mike.

This was no passive, friendly dog. It was intent on doing damage. Mike instinctively tried to grab at the dog's neck, but repeatedly, his hands were caught in between the dog's snapping teeth. His fingers, wrists and arms were being shredded by the sharp fangs and strong bites. Rolling his body over to protect his limbs and face from the ferocious animal, he grabbed a large stick that had been poking him in the back. As the dog mounted his back, trying to get to his neck, Mike pushed off his legs, stood up quickly, and bucked the dog from his back. Swinging the stick in front of him, he connected with the dog's head and sent him sprawling to the ground with a yelp.

Mike stumbled as he tried to race back to his car. He didn't know how much time he had. Luckily, no one saw him attack Miranda or her dog. When he got to his car, he searched through his bag and found an old t-shirt that he tore in half. He quickly wrapped each hand and arm with the shirt piece and tucked in the ends best he could. That was one mean, protective dog.

He returned to the front entrance of the park and found Miranda's car. Lying right on the front seat was a stack of file folders which probably had the reports he was looking for. The berm of the parking lot was edged with large rocks, so he picked up the largest he could find and smashed it into the window. He quickly grabbed the folders and left to search the Craig's house.

Miranda's house was on the corner of her street. He parked down the road and walked until he neared her backyard. The backyard was completely surrounded by trees and a fence which helped to shield him from nosy neighbors. Most people were at work now, so he should be clear to walk across her backyard and break into the sliding glass door on the deck. It only took him a few minutes to get in, look around and grab what paperwork or flash drives he could find.

He hadn't noticed his hands were starting to bleed again, leaving small drops of blood on their wooden floor.

Keslie Patch-Bohrod

CHAPTER 53

Maynard regained consciousness and struggled to his feet a few minutes after Mike left. He rose carefully and made his way down the ravine toward Miranda, still a bit groggy from the blow to his head. He nudged Miranda's arm with his snout and licked her face trying to wake her, but to no avail. He barked frenziedly.

Up in the maintenance shed, found near the main entrance, Nathan Fowler was attaching the snowplow to one of the county's trucks. Snow was expected and he needed this vehicle ready to plow the parking lots of the park, and the middle school across the way. The barking of a dog made him stop what he was doing. It sounded odd, not like a playful bark, but a Lassie bark, like something was wrong. It was a "Timmy's in the well" kind of bark he thought to himself, chuckling. He shook his head and kept working. The barking didn't stop.

Twenty years on the job told Nathan that few people used this park during the winter months. There were a couple of groups that came to the dog park in the morning to exercise their dogs. It had been too cold for most people to use the track for walking or running, and he wondered if maybe it was a stray or lost dog. He had better take a look just to play it safe. He cleaned his greasy hands with Gojo hand cleaner and wiped the residue on a towel. Checking to make sure his cell phone was in his pocket as well as his Swiss Army knife, he headed toward the park.

Immediately, he saw the dog staring down in the ravine, barking and racing back and forth. Nathan began to run knowing that something was definitely wrong.

"Hey boy, I'm here to help." Maynard moved out of the way and allowed Nathan to crawl down the ravine. He checked Miranda's pulse and pulled out his phone to call 911.

Keslie Patch-Bohrod

CHAPTER 54

"What do you mean you got pricked in the neck and thrown down a ravine? Jesus, Miranda, can't I leave you alone anymore?" Jack couldn't believe what he was hearing. He thought Miranda would be staying home behind locked doors with the security system engaged. But no, she had to go to an isolated dog park when people were going missing and possibly killed. "Do not leave the hospital until I get there, do you understand me?"

"Jack, I promise I won't leave. I need you to go to the park and get my car; it has important paperwork and flash drives that need to be given to John. Those reports may be the key to sorting out why all this is happening. Also, please stop at home and pick up my laptop so we can load the flash drive before John takes it. I want a chance to review it too."

"Miranda, who do you think knocked you out? Do you remember anything?" asked Jack.

"All I remember is being at the park with Maynard, dumping a poop bag in the trash and a man asking what kind of dog I had. When I opened my eyes, I was in the back of an EMS vehicle with a county employee holding my hand and holding Maynard's leash. He told me he found me because he heard the dog barking. After this is all done, we have to find him and take him to dinner as a thank you for saving me. Who knows when I would have been found? He is still with me, watching Maynard until you get here. His name is Nathan Fowler."

"Just sit tight Miranda, I will take care of the car, your stuff, contact John and thank Nathan."

Jack left Miranda in the care of the doctor and asked Nathan, her savior, for another favor. They drove back to the park, where Jack discovered Miranda's passenger window broken and none of the paperwork on the seat. As Maynard jumped into the back seat of the car, he asked Nathan to follow him back to the house in Jack's car. After parking Miranda's car in the garage and Maynard in the house, Jack drove Nathan back to the park's maintenance shed, thanking him profusely and promising to stay in touch.

On the way home, Jack called John Franklin. He asked if he had time to come to their house and outlined the details of the events of the day.

Knowing he had about thirty or forty minutes before John would arrive, Jack mentally ticked off a to-do list in his head as he drove home. First, feed and let out the dog, then call the hospital and check on Miranda's condition.

When Jack stepped into the house, Maynard was sitting in the hallway just outside of the kitchen area whining and staring at the floor. Did Maynard have an accident or maybe he threw up and then had eaten all the chunks? Upon closer inspection, Jack could see it looked more like blood. Maynard hadn't appeared severely hurt and no blood was obvious on his body. Miranda had been fine until she was attacked at the dog park. So, the only other scenario would be Miranda's attacker had come here searching for something, probably the rental records. But why was the person bleeding?

Careful not to step on the red puddle, he walked around to the side, grabbed Maynard's collar and led him to the sliding door that opened outside, noticing it was off its track. Jack knew enough about evidence not to go near it. He called John again and told him what he found and that someone must have been in the house, probably whoever attacked Miranda, looking for the apartment records.

"Jack, the last time I brought a team to your house was at the shore when Miranda was assaulted in the shower. I didn't like it then and I certainly don't like it now. I am getting involved in cases outside of my authority. I don't mind helping friends, but this is getting ridiculous!" shouted an exasperated John. "One thing I can say, life is definitely not dull being around you and Miranda."

As the forensic team dusted for prints and took samples of the blood, Jack and John struggled to repair the sliding glass door. Not being successful, Jack called his buddy Tony, who owned a construction company and told him what he needed done.

CHAPTER 55

Claude had found limited information about Mike in his extensive research, other than where he grew up, went to school and the few jobs that Mike had. Eddie Davis was another story. He was a two-time loser, spending ten years at East Jersey State Prison (previously known as Rahway State Prison) for aggravated assault. While there, he took advantage of college courses that Union County College offered inmates through its "Project Inside" program.

He was released and having completed an associate degree in computer programming, went to work for a small tech firm in Trenton. When his probation was finished, he left that company and struck out on his own, developing his illegal computer skills. He served another five years at New Jersey State Prison in Trenton. It wasn't until recently that he resurfaced as an associate of Mike O'Ryan. Claude found no employment records, FICA payments or indication how he was currently making a living.

John had passed along the medical report from the South Carolina police regarding Eddie's condition. He was in the critical care unit, suffering multiple, severe wounds to his face, arms and torso from the hungry wild boars. It was uncertain whether he would survive, and he had not been able to communicate with the physicians or the police since being rescued.

With that avenue cut off, Claude's only hope to figure out this mess was through the boiler room computers. Local police, once finding out his past occupation, put him on the case as a consultant. This legitimacy was critical not only in the chain of evidence but allowing him to do what was needed to obtain information. He would have to come up with a new alias after this. The police had already gathered up the closed-circuit television equipment that had been installed in the room. Apparently, whoever was running this shop had not trusted the workers. They were recorded and monitored to make sure they were using the agreed upon script, collecting the credit card and security code information accurately, then passing along the information in the prescribed way. What the police did not have was the CCTV digitized feed. That was probably on another computer in a second location. He would check Eddie Davis' house later in the day since he believed the other address on the invoice he found might be his. Right now, he had to look through the myriad of files and spreadsheets that outlined transactions the scammers had completed. He would also review the notebooks the scammers kept of the scripts they were to follow with each type of transaction. This was an incredibly detailed production and Claude was confident, that whoever was running the show kept records. These records would be the undoing of the nefarious group.

After spending the entire morning documenting and transferring files to a secured server for the police, Claude had identified most of the people who had been defrauded. Spreadsheets outlined the name, address, phone, credit card number, sometimes Social Security number and amount received from the victim along with the type of scam used. This was especially beneficial because if the authorities were able to find the money, they could return it in the end. This type of obsessive-compulsive behavior by criminals always surprised Claude. Why did they feel they had to keep records? They didn't pay taxes on these funds, and they certainly didn't pay payroll taxes to these workers. Was it just to feed their egos that they were able to scam this amount of money out of people? If the masterminds were monitoring the activities of the boiler room, they would know that the funds were being deposited into the specific accounts. It's like companies that keep two sets of books. What's the purpose? This is what gets them in trouble every time and makes life easy for law enforcement.

Claude called John Franklin and told him where he was headed and why.

CHAPTER 56

Mike O'Ryan was in a world of hurt. That dog had really done a number on his hands, arms and neck. Going to the hospital or a 'doc in the box' was out of the question so he had to take matters into his own hands if he could. The local CVS had what he needed: antiseptic, bandages and lighter fluid. He would try to clean up his wounds, then go to the apartment building's laundry room and set a fire.

Mike found it exceedingly difficult to drive a car with his hands wrapped in loads of gauze. The pain was almost unbearable at this point. Mike had to take six Advil, hoping it would help with the throbbing, intense aching. Since he only bought two cans of lighter fluid at CVS, he thought he should stop at Shop Rite in Somerville and buy more. You can never have too much accelerant. Plus, he could leave his car and walk over to the apartment, thus reducing his chances of being spotted or identified.

The Shop Rite was located behind Wolfgang's restaurant, bringing back the memory of the meeting with Greg back in the spring. Maybe it hadn't been such a great idea to get involved with his business, thought Mike; too late now. He went inside, found the aisle for the barbeque supplies and bought four more cans of lighter fluid. Thinking this could be a red flag to an overzealous cashier, he also loaded some charcoal briquettes, and for good measure four tablecloths. Those would come in handy to get the fire started. Thankfully, the stores still carried a large supply of these items for football tailgating parties.

He paid for his items, left the store and walked the short distance to the apartment back entrance. The stairs leading down to the laundry facility were empty, as was the laundry room. Mike unloaded his grocery bags, unwrapped the tablecloths and soaked them in lighter fluid. With another container of fluid, he doused the laundry room and the trash bins that were overflowing with debris. Mike pulled out his Bic lighter, lit a piece of paper sticking out of one of the trash bins, then quickly left the basement. He did the same in the rental office. As he slid into his car across the street in the parking lot, snow began to fall.

CHAPTER 57

As Claude was entering what he thought was Eddie Davis' house, he noticed snow beginning to accumulate on the sidewalk outside the front door. He stomped his feet a few times to remove any excess snow before entering the foyer. The rooms was sparsely furnished but did have a nice array of computer equipment. Claude was impressed. He quickly sat down at the table and fired up the devices. While he waited for the computer to run through its various tests, he scanned the house. It looked like no one actually lived there. There were no plants, no kitchen table and chairs, no mail and after getting up to look in the refrigerator, no food, just a couch, floor lamp and a couple of chairs. What gives, he thought? Maybe this was just a space for their monitoring computers.

He sat back down and began his work. In short order, he found the digital tapes of the boiler room, the documents outlining the lease arrangements for the boiler room and this house all tied to a company called Haverford Unlimited. Researching further showed a link to Mike O'Ryan. Spreadsheets for each month, dating back two years, showed lists of scam types, names, other identifying information and payments received. Those payments had been in the form of credit cards, gift cards (in this case they were focusing on Target and Walmart), Bitcoin and wire transfers. Then he hit pay dirt; the offshore accounts, account numbers and the amounts of money held in each.

Mike O'Ryan had used a number of scams: phishing emails, tech support, IRS/FBI scams, and Social Security. Claude thought he better check through any and all emails, searching for additional evidence for these types of scams. Included in the draft's section of the main email address, were letters and scripts that matched what he found in the boiler room. He also found several drafts from Allister Foley and Maybeth Roberts, thus tying Mike O'Ryan in with the disappearances of the tenants.

One last thing to check, thought Claude, the money transfers. Just to make sure Mike is the end point. There were several banks involved, and one interesting account in the name of Ernie Wannamaker. Could this be the main ringleader, thought Claude?

Easy enough to find out. Claude hacked into the account. Turned out to belong to an employee of a funeral home in Maryland. Sitting back in his chair and letting out a shout, Claude picked up his cell phone and called John Franklin.

"Hey John, I think we can get this wrapped up in short order. I have spreadsheets that will put Mike O'Ryan and Eddie Davis away for multiple counts of fraud and also allow the authorities to return funds to the victims. I am going to change the passwords on all the accounts so that the authorities will be the only people that can access them. I also have the name and address of an employee named Ernie Wannamaker, of the Hawthorne-Green Funeral Home in Columbia, Maryland. I would suggest someone go and pick him up for questioning. He has been receiving wire transfers in five thousand dollar increments, looking like payments for something. My guess, disposing of bodies."

John let out a whoop, "That is great news! I'll call Detective Morris and pass along the information. I am sure he'll put out an APB on Mike O'Ryan. We at least know where Eddie Davis is. Claude, let me call you back, Miranda is trying to reach me."

"Hey Miranda, I have some great news!"

"Before you get to that, we have a problem. The apartment building is on fire."

CHAPTER 58

Miranda had been sitting up in her hospital bed trying to convince the doctor to release her. All involved in her care, including Jack, were adamant that she remain overnight to be thoroughly evaluated. When her cell phone rang, she interrupted Jack who had been admonishing her for being irresponsible and not taking this whole situation as seriously as he thought she should.

"Jack, grab my phone out of my purse for me, it might be something important." Reluctantly, Jack got up from the bedside chair and fetched her phone.

Miranda looked at the number and said, "Oh my, my caller ID says it's the central alarm company. Hello, this is Miranda Craig."

"Ms. Craig, this is QRM Monitoring. We have a fire alarm going off on your property in Somerville and have called the fire department and local paramedics. They have sent multiple trucks and units; it appears to be quite a large fire."

"Thanks for calling me so quickly, we will get over there right away." Miranda disconnected her cell and looked at Jack and the doctor.

"I don't care what you say, I am leaving. There is a large fire at the apartment, and we need to get over there as soon as possible. I only hope that all the tenants were able to get out of the building safely."

Reluctantly, the doctor nodded, and Jack helped Miranda get dressed.

Following Miranda's phone call, John contacted Detective Morris and passed along the information collected by Claude, which proved who was responsible. He knew Mike O'Ryan was the main culprit, but also suspected, that O'Ryan might be the arsonist of the fire and wanted to make sure the word was out to all the officers in the vicinity to be on the lookout for him. He had found several pictures of Mike when researching his background and texted the most recent ones to Detective Morris. Thinking Mike might come to the house to transfer funds, destroy equipment or just to hide out,

John gave Morris the address and suggested he put the place under surveillance.

CHAPTER 59

Snow was piling up on the street and sidewalk, except for the area around the Craig's apartment building. The intense heat from the blaze and excess water from the pump trucks created a ring around the building. Luckily, all the tenants had been alerted to the fire by the central alarm in the building and were able to safely leave the property. Their belongings were not so lucky.

Standing outside the Starbucks, Miranda began to sob as she watched the firefighters diligently fighting the blaze. Jack put his arm around her and led her into the coffee shop. Something warm to drink and a place to sit and observe the chaos across the street would be cathartic. A few minutes later John Franklin joined them along with Detective Morris.

"Miranda, Jack- I am so sorry this is happening to you. Will they be able to save the building?" asked John as he sat down with his cup of coffee.

"It doesn't look like it. The Fire Marshall told us that he thinks it was set in the basement, but they will know more once they get the fire out and have the arson squad take a look. I just feel so bad for all the people who live there. Everything is gone! How could something like this happen? If this is arson, who could have done this?"

John looked over at Detective Morris who had joined them at the table. He nodded and the detective began to tell Miranda and Jack what he had learned from Claude's investigation.

"You mean Mike O'Ryan is responsible for all this, including the disappearance of those people?" bellowed Jack. Miranda put her hand on Jack's arm and gave it a gentle squeeze, reminding him that he was in a public place loaded with people.

"Yes. He and Eddie have been scamming people for a number of years and Claude discovered their current setup, including documents that detail who, what, where, when and how much money they swindled from these people. We believe they may have killed your three tenants, maybe more. There are police officers on their way to pick up a funeral home worker who may have helped them dispose of the bodies in some way. Other law enforcement people are trying to locate Mike. You two look worn out. Why don't you go home and try to get some sleep? There is nothing for you to do here other than fret and worry. We will check in with the fire chief and talk with you tomorrow. Jack, please make sure to put on your alarm."

"John, I'm not sure we can. My friend hasn't been able to get a replacement sliding door for us. He was coming out tonight to nail some boards in the opening but with all the snow, he can't get out until tomorrow. I guess I can bypass the door on the security system and pound a few two by fours into the frame with some Visqueen plastic sheeting to keep the snow out. It's going to be pretty cold in that kitchen when we wake up tomorrow!"

After scrounging around the garage and basement, Jack was able to find a large piece of plywood and several long two by fours. He grabbed the box of nails, found a hammer and began to cover the opening where the sliding glass doors were barely functional. The intruder had somehow removed them from their track and leaned them against the outside frame of the opening, crushing the track in the process. Thankfully, the piece of plywood was larger than the opening of the door. With the door resting outside on the frame, Jack began to pound nails into the two by fours and plywood on the inside. This would at least prevent some of the snow and cold air from entering the house. He could probably rig up a blanket over the plywood for extra insulation. Stepping back to admire his handiwork, all he could do was laugh. It looked ridiculous with the old blanket nailed onto the makeshift wall covering.

"Let's call HGTV and DIY Network!" exclaimed Miranda when she saw Jack's handiwork. "You most certainly won't win any carpentry awards. But I do have to hand it to you, no one is getting back through that door tonight without waking us up. We will have to take Maynard out through the front door or garage until Tony can get this thing fixed."

CHAPTER 60

Claude left Eddie's house after downloading and transferring all the files to a portable hard drive; he needed to deliver it to the police department as soon as possible. There were so many people who had been swindled out of large sums of money, and Claude was eager for them to find justice. He decided he would grab some dinner then return after dark. The rest of the house needed a thorough search; no telling what could be hidden in the floorboards, walls or garage.

With Eddie in critical condition in a South Carolina hospital, and the Craig apartment building engulfed in flames, Mike knew his days were numbered. He had to finish his business in Somerville and get all of the funds transferred to his offshore accounts. Thankfully, to his knowledge, no one knew of Eddie's place. He had warned Eddie not to use the address on any of his identification, to have packages or mail sent there or to even stay overnight.

Mike found his injury made movement more difficult, and the pain was increasing as the adrenaline wore off. He would have to rebandage his wounds soon; he seemed to be bleeding more. Mike had found it so thrilling setting the fire but knew it would be extremely dangerous to stay around and watch the excitement. Fire department officials actively scanned the onlookers knowing many arsonists watched the results of their work.

Blood was beginning to seep through the gauze and fibers of his long sleeve shirt and winter jacket. He worried that he might bleed out. Mike mumbled to himself, "I hope this blood loss isn't significant enough for me to lose consciousness, although I am feeling a bit lightheaded and nauseous. Maybe Eddie's friend in Maryland, the one that worked at the funeral home, might help me. They did have to stitch up cadavers after autopsies, so maybe he could suture the open wounds caused by the dog. There is no way I can drive down to Maryland in my present condition. Maybe, what's his name, Ernie, yeah that's it, Ernie could come up here. I could offer him an incentive. After he takes care of my arm, I can take care of him, so to speak. No use having that loose end."

Eddie's little hide away house was only a few miles from downtown Somerville. Mike had to force himself to stay focused while driving the short distance; his concentration kept waning. There was a short driveway to the left of the house that led to a single car garage in the back. Exiting the car, Mike turned the handle on the exterior of the garage door and pushed it up with what strength he had remaining. Slowly, he made his way back into the car and drove it carefully inside of the garage. After shutting the garage door, he made his way into the house through the back door. Everything was dark inside and with his vertigo, he was barely able to find a light switch. He stumbled to the thread bare couch in the living room. "I will just sit down here for a second, call Ernie, then begin transferring my money." With his last ounce of energy, he relayed what he needed Ernie to do, then passed out on the sofa.

Ernie grabbed a leather satchel, not unlike an old-fashioned doctor's bag and began to load instruments, sutures, scissors, bandages, antibiotics, and antiseptics. Even though this was a funeral parlor, it was well stocked with medicines and supplies. Someone was always getting cut or injured with all the sharp instruments and tools in this business. He quickly shut off the lights, locked the door, loaded up his car and began the three-hour drive to fix up Mike. That extra five grand he offered for this special service would sure come in handy.

It was about two in the morning when Ernie finally reached the house. There had been an accident on the New Jersey Turnpike that slowed him down for over an hour. He hoped Mike was alright. The way he had described his wounds and his condition caused Ernie to worry as to what he might find inside.

CHAPTER 61

The lead detective on the O'Ryan case insisted Claude walk him through all the evidence he had saved on the hard drive. Detective Morris wanted to make sure he understood every nuance of every scam and how the money could be recovered. Claude assured him that all the funds documented on the spreadsheets would be inaccessible to Mike O'Ryan or Eddie Davis. The passwords on all accounts had been changed, documented, and enclosed with the hard drive for the authorities. This was the only way Claude could ensure the funds would be returned to the victims and not into the hands of the criminals. He had also noted when, where, and who set up these previous passwords and what deposits were made and when. This correlated with the victims' names and data on the spreadsheets.

Claude told Detective Morris that he wanted to return to the house to do some more snooping. He was convinced there was more hiding under the surface. Detective Morris had other plans. There had been several murders over the past two days keeping the forensic technicians busy on those cases. As soon as the gruesome work was finished, they would be going over that property from top to bottom. Morris suggested Claude meet him there at eight the next morning. The technicians needed to know what he had touched, to exclude his prints from the investigation.

CHAPTER 62

Mike's body was draped over the corner of the sofa, with his bloody, left arm angled upward. Ernie hoped this position had helped stem some of the bleeding, as he began to check Mike's vitals. Heart rate and pulse slow, breathing labored, and a deadly pallor. Chances are, he's in hypovolemic shock, deduced Ernie as he pulled his stethoscope from his ears. Carefully removing the blood-soaked coat and shirt, he began to assess the damage and consider his next steps. Depending on how much blood Mike lost, would determine if he would need a transfusion. Ernie was type O negative, which was the universal donor blood type. How fortunate for Mike, thought Ernie. I can be the transfusion source without knowing his blood type.

"Oh Mike, what a mess you are in. I guess I better introduce myself, I'm Ernie Wannamaker and I am here to save your ass. I don't know if you can hear me, but I am going to tell you everything that I will be doing to help. Remember you are going to pay me five thousand dollars for doing this today. After I put on a pair of surgical gloves, I am going to rinse your wounds with a saline solution." As he was spraying the liquid on Mike's arm, he continued to explain his actions.

"You have lost quite a bit of blood from these dog bites. I don't understand why you just did not go to the emergency room to have this looked at and treated. Dog bites are serious and dirty, you could sue the owners of that vicious animal for this. So now, I am going to pat the area dry and look at the damage. This wound looks quite deep; however, I don't think it reached the bone. The skin has been torn and ripped by the dog's teeth. You are going to need a bunch of stitches to close this wound effectively; it is not going to look pretty."

Ernie pulled out his suture kit and moved the floor lamp closer to the couch to better light his work area. "Since this wound is deep and will need a lot of stitches, I am going to inject some Lidocaine to numb the area." He retrieved the sterile needle from his bag along with a small vial. Retracting the plunger to fill the syringe, he pushed a tiny amount of the liquid out to expel any air bubbles, and plunged the needle several times around the wound, thoroughly numbing the entire area. Even though Mike was unconscious, he did not want to take a chance that he would awaken and jerk his body while Ernie was mending his wounds.

"I think interrupted sutures will be best, because of the uneven edges." Picking up the sterilized needle driver, he locked the needle in place. Using the tissue forceps to push down on the side of wound, he inserted the needle at the proper angle, then lined up the other side and brought the needle up and through. Separating the needle from the driver, he reattached it on the other side, pulling the needle through the skin. Quick wraps around the needle holder with the suture created an overhand knot. He tightened the threads to make sure the skin lined up properly and finished his knot with a second and third throw, reversing direction to tie off the suture. "One down and maybe fifty to go!"

Ernie worked steadily for the next forty-five minutes continuing the suture process, wiping the wound and then determining the placement of the next stitch. When he was done, he surveyed his work and announced he was finished. However, he was still worried about Mike's pallor.

"Buddy, I think you are going to need some blood, too. I can't go to a blood bank right at this moment, so you have to get some of mine without the anticoagulant. After I start an intravenous line, I will draw off a bag of my blood, then give it to you through the IV.

Ernie applied a tourniquet to Mike's right arm and swabbed the area with an alcohol wipe. He inserted the IV catheter along the line of the vein that had been exposed, and slowly advanced it and the needle into the vein. Removing the needle, he attached a three-way stopcock and secured the catheter with tape. Tourniquet released, the IV tubing attached to the stopcock, and the other end to the saline bag. After adjusting the flow, Ernie began the process of drawing his blood.

First, he put on clean, sterile gloves, then tied the tourniquet to his left arm, tightening it with his right hand and teeth. He swabbed the area with an alcohol wipe and picked up a needle that he connected to a tube that led to the bag where it would be collected. Ernie hoped one pint would be sufficient for Mike to regain consciousness. It was all about the transfer of funds. He needed the passwords and account numbers from Mike otherwise this night would be a total waste of time. When the bag was full, he switched it to the IV line and adjusted the flow. He guessed about an hour should do it.

While he waited for Mike to come around, he cleaned his instruments, put all the needles in a special 'sharps' container and the miscellaneous trash into a garbage bag. All surfaces were wiped with the remaining alcohol pads. It was starting to get light out, and he had to get this show on the road.

Just as he was returning from loading his car, Mike began to stir.

"Wakey, wakey, eggs and bakey!" Ernie sang. Mike mumbled a few words and opened his eyes. Not knowing where he was or why he was in such pain, he leapt off the couch knocking the IV stand to the floor.

"Easy does it Mike. I have been stitching you up and you lost a lot of blood; I had to give you a pint. Just lay back down, you need to rest."

Mike did as he was told, looking around the room. The events of the previous day came back to him: finding the files and hard drive in Miranda's car, being attacked by the dog, ransacking her house, setting fire to the apartment building. "Hey, man. I really owe you big time."

"Yes, you do. So, I would appreciate it if you would transfer the five grand for me so I can get back to Maryland."

Mike tried to sit up again, groaning. "I don't think I can sit up and do that, but maybe I can walk you through it on the computer over there."

Ernie thought for a minute. "I guess that will be alright." Ernie walked over to the desk, turned on the computer and sat down in the chair with his back to Mike. He was concerned that Mike was behind him but there really wasn't another option. Loss of blood made Mike weak. As the computer warmed up, he thought of what he would do with all of the money he would be receiving shortly. The computer completed all of its tests and the sign on screen came up. Mike gave him the password and told him to click on the right file folder.

"Hey, what gives Mike? There is nothing in this file folder. There is no spreadsheet, there is no Word document, there is nothing!"

Mike gingerly sat up on the couch and said, "What the hell are you talking about? There should be a detailed spreadsheet with account numbers and dollar amounts listed. That would tell me what account I can draw the five thousand dollars from to pay you. Are you sure you opened up the right file folder?"

"I opened up the one you told me to. How about if I look around at some of the other folders you have shown here and see if maybe someone put it in the wrong place?"

Ernie grew increasingly aggravated as he opened and closed the various file folders on the computer finding nothing. Fighting back his rage, he noticed Mike too, was getting agitated. Thinking Mike planned to scam him, Ernie reached into his pocket and pulled out the syringe that he had gotten from his car earlier. He was not going to let Mike get away with this. Also, he was worried that all the killing that Mike and Eddie had done might eventually lead to him so the most expeditious way to manage this would be to kill Mike, get out of there quickly, then cover his tracks.

Mike too was thinking similar thoughts and assumed that while he was unconscious Ernie had somehow logged onto the computer and transferred all of the data to another location. He could not allow Ernie to get away with that. Mike saw Ernie get up from the chair and turned toward him with a syringe in his hand. "Hey, what the hell are you doing?"

Ernie, thinking quickly, said "Oh nothing, this is an anticoagulant that you are going to need with the pint of blood that I gave you. It will stop you from bleeding out because your wounds are still somewhat open and seeping. Mike did not believe him. As Ernie came closer to the IV stand, Mike fired the handgun that he had buried in the cushions of the sofa. The shot hit home but failed to stop Ernie. He was able to grab the gun away from Mike and inject a formaldehyde solution into the IV bag and turn on the regulator. Within seconds the drug cursed through Mike's veins and began to render him unconscious. Death would follow soon.

CHAPTER 63

Claude arrived at the police station a few minutes early for the eight o'clock meeting with Detective Morris. He was anxious to get back to the house and do a more thorough search because he believed there was much more to find. At precisely eight a.m., Detective Morris came out of the station and motioned for Claude to join him in his police vehicle. The forensic team would be meeting them at the house shortly. When they arrived the team's van was parked in the driveway and the technicians were unloading their equipment from the open door of the vehicle. Claude noted there was another car in the driveway that had not been there earlier. This put Detective Morris on high alert, and he motioned to the technicians to get behind the van while he did a search of the house to make sure no one was inside. Detective Morris went around to the back of the house quietly and entered through the kitchen. Doing a sweep with his gun, he cleared each room as he made his way to the living room. He immediately froze with his gun drawn when he saw two men, one lying on the couch and the other lying on the floor presumably dead. Rushing over, he checked each body's pulse points to determine their status. It was hard to tell if there was a pulse. Letting out a deep breath and holstering his gun, he opened the front door and called to the forensic team to begin their work and reminded them to include the garage. He also pulled out his cell phone and made a call to the paramedics just in case.

"Boy it's a real shit show in there Claude! I am going to have you stay out here until we can process the house. Both men are in real bad shape and may be dead, one is Mike O'Ryan and who knows who the other guy is."

The paramedics arrived a few minutes later and began their work. Both men were barely alive and needed to be transported to the nearest trauma center as soon as possible. Using stretchers, they loaded the men in their rig and rushed off, lights flashing and sirens wailing.

Morris got on the phone again and called the precinct to arrange for police guards to be stationed at the bedside of both men; he wasn't going to let either one of them get away.

CHAPTER 64

Miranda was so excited to have her son Kevin home from London where he had been studying finance for the fall semester. Erica, their daughter, would be driving home from her college tomorrow after her exams. The past few months had been so hectic and horrible, that Miranda was really looking forward to a quiet holiday down at the shore with her family. The deaths of the tenants and the total destruction of their apartment building weighed heavily on Miranda's conscience. She knew there was nothing she could do about what happened, but nevertheless she felt somewhat responsible.

Thankfully, Greg Baker and Celia Ravenscroft survived their ordeal and were back hard at work handling Greg's multiple properties.

As she and Jack were sitting down to dinner that night, John Franklin called to update them on the status of the case. Eddie Davis had not survived his wild boar attack and died in the hospital in South Carolina from his wounds. The other man found in Eddie Davis' house was identified as Ernie Wanamaker, an employee of a Funeral Home in Maryland. He had recovered from his gunshot wound and confessed to the alkaline hydrolysis of four people. He was offered a deal to reduce his sentence if he turned state's evidence against Mike O'Ryan, who had also survived. Wannamaker identified three of the victims as the missing tenants and the fourth body belonged to a man named Harry, who he believed was O'Ryan's former business partner. The forensic team found DNA in the freezer in Eddie Davis' garage that belonged to Harry Murphy.

"Claude has been working nonstop, not only with the Somerset County officials, but also with the FBI and other law enforcement agencies to identify the workers employed in Mike O'Ryan's boiler room. The scammers are still being rounded up and will be charged with appropriate crimes. Claude is helping them identify many of the victims of Mike O'Ryan's scams and Internet frauds. Authorities will be returning most, if not all, of the money back to the victims. Mike will be facing numerous criminal charges that include internet fraud, mail fraud, attempted murder, and four counts of murder. Chances are he will be rotting in jail for the rest of his life. Too bad New Jersey no longer has the death penalty. By the way, the last time a prosecutor even came close to a death penalty conviction was in 1985. A young Union County Prosecutor nailed eleven of twelve votes. That kid lawyer could not sway that last juror- must have been a religious fanatic."

"John, I don't know about you, but I am looking forward to several weeks in Loveladies where I expect absolutely nothing to happen. I hope I'm not like Jessica Fletcher in the TV show *Murder She Wrote.* Wherever she goes she runs into murder of some kind. It hasn't even been a year and I have come in contact with at least seven murders. I hope this is the last of it. Our kids are coming home, and we are driving to the shore in a couple of days to spend the Christmas holiday. I hope you and Lori will be able to come down and have Christmas dinner with us and put an end to all of this mess."

CHAPTER 65

Long Beach Island
Christmas Day 2018

Miranda had been cooking all day. John and Lori were set to come over at four o'clock to help them celebrate Christmas. After the table had been set and the wine glasses put out, Miranda began to put the finishing touches on the meal. They would start with a shrimp ceviche followed by a garlic studded standing rib roast, scalloped potatoes and roasted asparagus. Of course, Jack had many bottles of Amizetta Complexity Cabernet Blend ready to be uncorked and consumed. As they would sit down to dinner, Miranda would put her bread pudding in the oven, that way it would be ready when they were finished eating. She would melt a small amount of vanilla ice cream and mix a tablespoon or two of Wild Turkey bourbon as a sauce for the bread pudding. Their friends could also scoop vanilla ice cream on top to really add to the calories.

After finishing such a large dinner, most decided to take a stroll down the street. Luckily there had been no snow for a while and the roads were clear. The temperature outside was in the upper forties making it relatively comfortable for a Christmas week.

Miranda decided to stay behind and take her glass of red wine and Maynard out to the dock. She sat on the steps leading down to the lower level and gazed at the clean lagoon water. The sun was at its lowest spot on the horizon. She could hear Django Reinhardt picking away on the Pink Martini radio station from the Sonos inside the house. The lagoon was as still as the dead, and Miranda found herself imagining that she was somewhere else. It definitely did not feel or look like New Jersey. She thought to herself, 'How can somewhere this quiet and beautiful be New Jersey? During the summer, the gardens were all in bloom with crape myrtles, hydrangeas, and geraniums looking more like a Parisian countryside, or the canals of Venice, than the Jersey Shore.'

The sun set swiftly at the end of the lagoon with a plop, calling an end to the day, and hopefully to this grim chapter in their lives. It was normally bleak, cold and empty this time of year but the quiet now was especially welcome. She would look forward to the next few weeks of boredom and imagine the Loveladies ennui setting in again!

Miranda and Jack so desperately needed this break in their daily routine to regroup and engage with one another. The New Year for sure would bring new challenges and new problems, but surely with the love and support of family and friends, they would get through it just like they had gotten through these past few crazy months.

Hearing her family and friends returning from outside, Miranda picked up her wineglass and began the walk back into the house. Alarmingly, Maynard lowered his head and let out a slow rumbling growl which signaled to Miranda that something was amiss. Turning one hundred and eighty degrees, she caught sight of Alina Pronin, her neighbor across the lagoon, looking at her. As she recalled what happened during the summer, a profound sense of sadness filled Miranda knowing that Alina was alone this Christmas. In an effort to be a good neighbor, Miranda waved and wished her a Merry Christmas as she slowly trudged back into the house.

Alina took out her cell phone and made a call to her superiors.

Stay tuned for the third Miranda Craig thriller taking place in Loveladies, New Jersey.

AUTHOR BIOGRAPHY

Keslie Patch-Bohrod grew up in Ravenna, Ohio. After graduate school, she lived and worked in Orlando, Florida; Macon, Georgia; Atlanta, Georgia; Cranbury, New Jersey; and New York City. Presently, she lives in Warren, New Jersey with her husband Bill and their dog Bo while summers are spent in Loveladies, New Jersey with their adult children Jaysen and Stephanie.

Contact the author at loveladiesennui@gmail.com and visit her website at https://kesliebohrod.wixsite.com/loveladiesennui Please like, share and follow her on Facebook and Instagram @kesliebohrod

Keslie Patch-Bohrod

Starry Night Publishing

Everyone has a story...

Don't spend your life trying to get published! Don't tolerate rejection! Don't do all the work and allow the publishing companies to reap the rewards!

Millions of independent authors like you are making money, publishing their stories now. Our technological know-how will take the headaches out of getting published. Let Starry Night Publishing take care of the hard parts, so you can focus on writing. You simply send us your Word Document, and we do the rest. It really is that simple!

The big companies want to publish only "celebrity authors," not the average book-writer. It's almost impossible for first-time authors to get published today. This has led many authors to go the self-publishing route. Until recently, this was considered "vanity-publishing." You spent large sums of your money to get twenty copies of your book, to give to relatives at Christmas just so you could see your name on the cover. However, the self-publishing industry allows authors to get published in a timely fashion, retain the rights to your work, keeping up to ninety percent of your royalties instead of the traditional five percent.

We've opened up the gates, allowing you inside the world of publishing. While others charge you as much as fifteen-thousand dollars for a publishing package, we charge less than five-hundred dollars to cover copyright, ISBN, and distribution costs. Do you really want to spend all your time formatting, converting, designing a cover, and then promoting your book because no one else will?

Our editors are professionals, able to create a top-notch book that you will be proud of. Becoming a published author is supposed to be fun, not a hassle.

At Starry Night Publishing, you submit your work, we create a professional-looking cover, a table of contents, compile your text and images into the appropriate format, convert your files for eReaders, take care of copyright information, assign an ISBN, allow you to keep one-hundred-percent of your rights, distribute your story worldwide on Amazon, Barnes and Noble and many other retailers, and write you a check for your royalties. There are no other hidden fees involved! You don't pay extra for a cover or to keep your book in print. We promise! Everything is included! You even get a free copy of your book and unlimited half-price copies.

In nine short years, we've published more than four thousand books, compared to the major publishing houses, which only add an average of six new titles per year. We will publish your fiction or non-fiction books about anything and look forward to reading your stories and sharing them with the world.

We sincerely hope that you will join the growing Starry Night Publishing family, become a published author, and gain the world-wide exposure that you deserve. You deserve to succeed. Success comes to those who make opportunities happen, not those who wait for opportunities to happen. You just have to try. Thanks for joining us on our journey.

www.starrynightpublishing.com

www.facebook.com/starrynightpublishing/

Made in the USA
Monee, IL
28 January 2022

90128174R00125